A GRAIN OF WHEAT.

A
GRAIN OF WHEAT

by

TOYOHIKO KAGAWA

TRANSLATED BY MARION R. DRAPER
EDITED BY GLENN CLARK

HARPER & BROTHERS *Publishers*
NEW YORK AND LONDON
1936

CONTENTS

A GRAIN OF WHEAT

Often Kakichi would go down to the water's edge and drag out an extra log or two. (p. 1)

"Why not come over and join us? We have more rice than we need." (p. 25)

These and the following illustrations are from the Japanese motion picture, "A Grain of Wheat." Courtesy of Toyohiko Kagawa.

"What do you mean when you say you are God's child?"
Kakichi asked the hermit.   (p. 37)

"Dear Kakichi, we will be sorry to have you leave us
and will think of you often."   (p. 54)

Kakichi and Yoshie walked very slowly.　(p. 97)

"There has been no one who could assume leadership,"
said the mill owner.　(p. 110)

A letter had come from Yoshie.   (p. 112)

There were days when Kakichi was obliged to stay at home to nurse his father.   (p. 122)

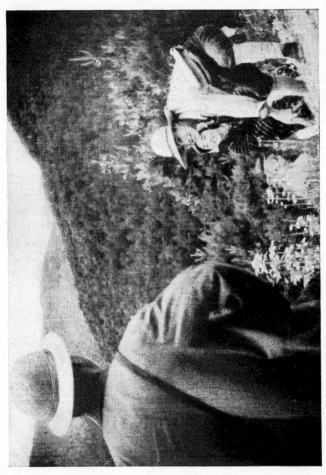

By the middle of December, with Yoshie's assistance, they had planted twenty-five acres. (p. 122)

Yoshie made a new dress for Yuriko.   (p. 127)

The sergeant handed Kakichi a telegram. (p. 140)

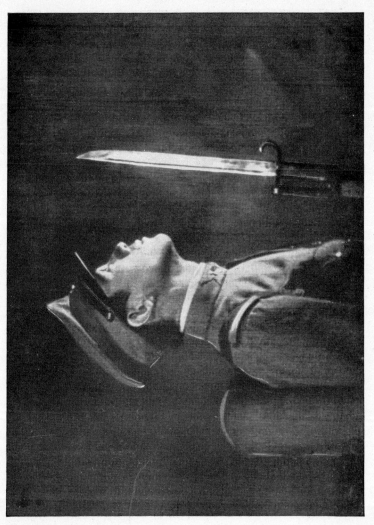

Here was a dream all men might unite in dreaming, a prayer all might pray.   (p. 138)

"Except a grain of wheat fall into the ground and die, it abideth alone."

(p. 145)

CHAPTER I

THE TEMPTATIONS OF TWILIGHT

IT WAS KAKICHI'S WORK TO BREAK UP THE RAFTS WHICH CAME floating down the Toyo River and drag the wet logs up on the sandy banks. It was work that he loved. The river held enchantment for him, and from its steady flow he would lift his young eyes to the far hills and feel a momentary stilling of the unrest that burned so furiously within his breast. The mountains in the far distance were wrapped in pearly mist, while in the foreground the mulberry fields, seared with frost and interspersed here and there with patches of small, dwarfed pines, turned the surface of the land an ashen gray. The sky, of a gloomy leaden color, overhung the humid plain which surrounded the village of Toyohashi. Through this plain flowed the Toyo River, and its waters were a deep, clear blue, as though they had been dyed with indigo.

Rather than loiter around the lumberyard, to be scolded by the garrulous foreman who was forever ranting at Kakichi for his indolence, he would go down to the water's edge and drag out an extra log or two. As he tugged at the big, wet logs with his mates they sang together, and there was something in that singing that Kakichi liked, although he rarely joined his voice with theirs.

> "Heave ho! All together!
> A long pull and a strong pull!
> The mountains are snow-covered,

I

> This year's a year of plenty.
> Our house will prosper, with treasures heaping,
> Filling the storehouse.
> A long pull and a strong pull,
> Heave ho! All together!"

He liked the words, but they did not, he thought morosely, apply to him. His home was far distant, across the mountains. It was a poor home, and it had been years since he had been there. He was lucky to have a job, however discontented he was at it.

In Maruhachi's lumberyard there were only two full-time lumbermen, and Kakichi, by virtue of the five years during which he had been employed here, was one of these. But when a big raft came down the river, seven or eight shoresmen were called in to help, and they would plunge into the cold water, splashing and singing in loud, lusty tones, and heaving and tugging the logs to the shore. But their chief enjoyment was ridiculing Kakichi. Ushitaro, a great strong fellow from the village down the river, was their leader.

"Well, Kakichi!" he would gibe, "quite a man you're getting to be these days, spending your nights out."

Kakichi stood still, hearing the raucous laughter of his fellows, and keeping his brown eyes fastened upon a school of small carp darting hither and thither in the clear water of a shallow current out beyond the logs. His face reddened, and their derisive laughter tightened his anger into a small, hard knot in his breast. How did they know? he wondered dully.

"Oh, I saw you, dodging in and out of that dark street at the Quarter," Ushitaro pursued, his thick lips curled in a smile at the boy's confusion.

"Well," said another, "when a man is twenty, it is time

he should be wanting a wife, and it is these silent ones like Kakichi who find the pretty ones. Come, tell us about it," and their voices joined in the urging.

But Kakichi's young face was masked in its customary sullen taciturnity. He said nothing. He was no different from the rest of them, he thought angrily, defensively, and he should be able to recount his experiences as they did their own. He both envied them and hated them: envying them the heartiness and ease of their manner, hating their roughness and coarseness and the stories they were forever telling him and each other, and the filthy pictures they had to show. He had bought some of them and they were hidden in the bottom of the small willow basket where he kept his pitifully few clothes, but even this had not succeeded in making him one of them. In the face of their experienced composure he was always hatefully uncomfortable.

He had always been shy, talking hesitantly or, more often, not at all. It was, he thought, perhaps because he had been brought up in the mountains where he had been sent at the age of ten to work as errand boy in another lumber camp. He had been shoved around by older men and laughed at ever since he could remember. He had found silence to be a far better defense than any words, even had he been able to think of adequate words with which to meet derision. In consequence, he had earned the reputation of being a dull-witted fellow and had been treated as such, so that with the passing of the years he had scarcely improved his conversational abilities. It was true enough that he had little education, for his father had sent him away to earn his living before there had been an opportunity to learn. He was careless, too, of his personal appearance, but it had scarcely seemed worth while to be otherwise. His wages were pitifully small; they afforded him amusement and there was none left with which to buy clothes. Besides, no one cared.

It was small wonder, he thought, that he spent his nights out, and he would have liked to tell them so. The tiny shack in the back of the lumber camp where he lived was unbearably hot in the summertime and stank of fish from the river. In the winter it was cold and damp, and he had to sleep in his clothes to keep warm. The little house where he went each evening was better than that. It had a sign of red cloth hanging from its low eaves, and in the front room there was a shop, where wine was sold, and tobacco. When he came into the shop, the girl behind the counter would leave it and go away with him into the dark rooms at the back. There were other girls, but he liked the one in the shop. Her face was painted and hard; her eyes were as black as the darkness of the hot room. She had taken some of the money he had given her to buy perfume. It was strong and pungent, and the odor of it clung to all his clothes and sometimes made him feel sick.

Yes, he should, he thought, talk of these things with the others, but somehow he could not. He hated his shyness. He was oppressed by it. It interfered with his work. The one thing that he disliked exceedingly was being sent around every month to collect outstanding accounts of the company. But his employer trusted him, so he had no option in the matter; he must go. He did not actually mind collecting the money; it was having to argue with people who did not want to pay that he dreaded. He couldn't argue; he couldn't find any persuasive words. Last month he had come back without getting the money from three of his customers and Maruhachi had berated him angrily.

"It is because you are always so sullen," he ranted loudly, not caring who heard. "Of course, it's a bad thing to talk too much, but it's a great deal worse not to be able to say what's necessary to be said. I cannot see why I continue to keep anyone so worthless. You know," he added, "they say that when a man is speechless, it is because his father's tongue is numbed from the drinking of wine. Is that true?" But Kakichi, in shame, did not answer. It was true, and that it might be the cause of his silence and stupidity was beyond bearing. But thought of all this, and of the men's jeering and mocking laughter, could be lost . . . yes, must be lost, when the lights of the city brightened the sky and the day's work was ended.

Then, when the evening mist hung low over the silvered surface of the river, and Kakichi had performed his last task of fastening the logs securely to a raft so they would not float away, he would hurry away from the camp, through the narrow winding streets that led to the licensed quarter, not three blocks away, and to the girl who kept the shop.

In the beginning he had gone only occasionally, but for the last months he had gone every night, always curiously seeking a release that was forever eluding him, and spending in a short time his entire month's salary, until, as on this particular evening, when he wanted more than ever to go, there was no more to spend. He walked the streets idly, restlessly, hating this poverty and everything about his life. It was ugly and his thin face was distorted with its ugliness.

And then, as he walked, quite suddenly he thought of a way by which he could secure some money.

It was still early, and he turned a few blocks to the west to a shop where wooden boxes were made. There was a bill, here, to be collected. He knocked on the door and the shopkeeper's wife opened it almost at once. He had come to collect the five-yen bill due his company, he told her, speaking quickly. She hesitated.

"I know it's late," he interrupted, pushing back the fear in his breast. "But I am on my way home and was told not to come without it."

She went into the house and returned with the money, which he took, hurrying away from the door. Would he not put his seal on her account book? she inquired, calling after him.

"I haven't it with me," Kakichi evaded. "I'll bring it along later."

It had been easy; it would be easy. When next he was paid he would return it with the accounts he had collected. He should have thought of this before. And he hurried away in the gathering darkness.

But when next he was paid he owed the girl in the shop a considerable amount, and it seemed better to wait until the next time. And the next time it began to seem unlikely that he would be discovered and the necessity for money was greater than ever. The girl in the shop was an obsession, the path to her door easy to take. And yet some day, he knew with an uneasy certainty, the five-yen note must be repaid or his theft would be detected.

It was on a sunny autumn day that the foreman called Kakichi and sent him out to collect the bill from the box store. It had, he complained, gone too long unpaid. Kakichi's mind was now occupied with an immediate way in which the money could be returned. He walked slowly, thoughtfully, away from the lumberyard. The sky was so very clear and the sun shone down upon him as though it would penetrate to the very core of his being. He raised an unsteady hand to wipe off his face.

He had never been in prison, and stealing was a prison offense. Maruhachi was not the kind of man who might overlook a thing of this kind. And, once in prison, there would be no one to plead for him, to find a way out for him. He passed by the boxmaker's, and making a complete circle, came back again to Maruhachi's by the same road, the problem still unsolved. It was another two weeks until payday. His heart was heavy and distressed, his mind frightened and filled with foreboding. How they would laugh when they knew!

He approached the foreman hesitantly. "The master of the shop was not at home," he lied, not meeting the man's eyes.

"You can go back to-morrow. This account is long overdue."

But, for some reason, probably because this was a busy season, it was for the moment forgotten. Kakichi considered working at Yamasa's . . . a lumber company not far away. They paid higher wages, and it would be easy enough there, with thirty yen a month, to pay a small debt of five. But he knew that he would not go; he had been at Maruhachi's too long. Besides, they would find him there, too.

The stories of the men bored him, now. They were always of money or of women, and the pictures they handed about among themselves he looked at without seeing.

The waters of the river had grown colder; the crabs hid themselves, and the green moss, which clung to the gray stone walls near the bridge, withered up. And each night Kakichi took the same road, going more stealthily now since even his master's wife had chided him lately for his restlessness. He went quickly, too, passing by the priests and the Christians who often held services on the street at the four corners at the gate of the licensed quarter. Kakichi had never had any religious teaching, and he did not pause now to hear what they might say. He thought, rather disdainfully, that these men were probably skilled at getting money, with their preaching. That was all men wanted, anyway, and they were no different. And they called it Christianity! A dangerous teaching, surely, for the people of Japan. And foolish! And he passed them by.

But crossing the last street, he had, by necessity, to go around a crowd that had gathered about a fortuneteller who harangued loudly from the sidewalk. Kakichi peered across at the man, curiously. He had long black hair and eyes like charcoal, and whatever he was saying must have been amusing because the small crowd gathered about him laughed continually. Suddenly the man fastened his eyes on Kakichi.

"Now there," he said loudly, to Kakichi's dismay pointing him out, "there's an unusual face. Step forward, young fellow!" And the crowd pushed him forward, despite his endeavors to move on.

"Here," pursued the dark man, "are the features of one who will make his mark in this world." And the eyes of all of them centered upon Kakichi's sullen face. He moved away from a restraining arm, and yet he was as though spellbound, listening to the voice above his head.

"Now, gentlemen," the fortuneteller was saying, "this face is an example of the resolute physiognomy which I was explaining to you just now. This young man is silent and self-possessed, extremely persevering in his work . . . and still . . . and still . . ." He paused, and Kakichi listened, frightened, entranced, held by the man's narrow black eyes.

"There is some weakness here . . . if I examine him closely I can discover what secrets he holds in his inmost heart. For there are secrets there . . . his eyes hold them."

Kakichi felt cold, and moved uneasily from one foot to another, pressed in by those on both sides who stared at him curiously and, he thought, knowingly. There would surely be someone in this crowd who knew him, he thought fear-fully. And still he could not go. "This fortuneteller knows everything," he thought weakly. "He knows about the five yen I stole and the pictures at the bottom of the basket. There is nothing he does not know about me!"

The gaslight on the corner burned with a buzzing sound. The faces of the crowd, in the dim light of the lamp, were thrown into sharp relief as if they were figures on a print. Pointed, curious, impersonal faces. The fortuneteller leaned forward and put his finger beneath Kakichi's chin, looking down at him directly. Kakichi lowered his eyes.

"A man who keeps looking down will surely be lost, but one who looks up will make his way in this world. What should you fear? Keep your eyes on the sky."

Kakichi swallowed and was silent. His throat ached with his wish to be gone, to crawl away through the crowd. He had no will; they were right when they taunted him with weakness.

"Your father is a drunkard," the man continued, and Kakichi drew in a quick, frightened breath. "Hold out your hands." Someone next to him shoved out his hands. He held them still, not knowing why he obeyed.

"You have five brothers and sisters. That's right, isn't it?" Kakichi looked up at the man, suddenly, in astonishment and gave a single nod of assent, fascinated. "If you yield to temptation you will be another Goemon Ishikawa." There was loud laughter from the crowd. Ishikawa was a great robber, as famous in Japan as Captain Kidd was in Ameri-can legends. But at this laughter Kakichi fled precipitately, going back quickly to his shed in the lumberyard. What things that man might not have revealed! If he had known that his father was a drunkard, and that he had five brothers and sisters, then he knew about the five yen. He knew that one of his sisters was a dancing girl, and one a prostitute. He was probably, even now, telling these things to those who stood and listened. And on the morrow, surely, even if all these things were not known, he would be sent to collect the money from the boxmaker. All these fears pressed in upon him in quick succession, yet the last was the greatest. He could contrive no further evasions about that. It seemed to him suddenly, in his young fright and bewilderment, in the uncertainty that marked all his actions, that there was nowhere to turn to. Other men had homes, families; he had nothing. The need for that home which he had not seen for years was suddenly imperative. He went to his room and took out a padded kimono and an old lined one and wrapped them in paper. Taking them quickly to a shop on the next street, he got a few coins in return. It would not, he knew, be enough to take him home. But it would help. For he was going home.

There was the problem of what he should say to his master, for he could not leave him without a valid excuse. He lay awake all through the night considering this, and in the morning very early sent a telegram addressed to himself and purporting to come from his mother, saying that his father was very ill and he was needed at once.

It was delivered to him while he worked on the river bank, where he had lifted his eyes from the logs to watch a great flock of white cranes pass overhead. He took the telegram from the clerk's hand and opened it.

"Has something happened, Kakichi?" the man asked in sincere concern. Yes, Kakichi lied stolidly, something had happened. His father was dangerously ill and he must go home at once. Kakichi started quickly up the hill towards the office, the clerk following murmuring something that Kakichi did not wait to hear. He had only one impulse and that was to be gone, and quickly. It was, in reality, a flight.

CHAPTER II

BEFORE THE DAWN

THE TRAIN PUFFED ITS WAY NORTH ALONG THE BANKS OF THE Toyo River, but because he had not enough money to ride all the way, Kakichi had to walk from the village of Nagashino, a distance of twenty-three miles. But this, he reflected as he plodded wearily along, was probably a part of his punishment. He would never go back to Maruhachi's, he decided as he walked. He might, if his father would help him, have a small lumber business of his own in his own home town. But this did not seem very likely. Or he might, he thought as he looked up at the bare slopes of the hills lying waste, cultivate some of that land for his living. But he would never go back.

In the valleys the forest birds were singing, and a long string of cart horses went by on the road, drawing their heavy loads, reminding Kakichi of how he as a little fellow had clung to the backs of such carts when he went back and forth to neighboring villages. That had been a long time ago. So much might have happened at home. They had always been poor, and if the little hardware shop that his mother kept had not prospered, and if his father still spent the few coins that they saved for wine, it was very possible that they might not have even enough rice to feed him. They might not be glad to see him. Perhaps he ought not to go.

His steps lagged, and his feet ached painfully as, at eight o'clock the next evening, he climbed the last hill. He was very hungry, too, and so cold that he shivered. The mountains of this North country are over three thousand feet above sea level, and the tops are covered with snow.

The little town was changed . . . there were more electric lights, more people hurrying on the streets. He did not seem to know any of them. Along the side of the road a little brook flowed down to the lower village, and followed along this same road to the foothills. On a corner of this road, on a corner opposite the brook, stood Kakichi's home. He paused in front of it. It was small and brown, with low-hanging eaves, and wide shutters all across the front to cover the shopwindows at night. These had not yet been put up and a single dim electric bulb lit up the interior of an empty shop. He was suddenly reluctant to enter; it all seemed strange. But he was very tired and he longed, as a child, to sleep for just one night at least in his old home. So he slipped around into the little open court of the kitchen and entered the door.

The first thing he saw was his father's brown, wrinkled face regarding him in a startled fashion from above a wine-cup.

The furnishings of the room seemed even poorer than he had remembered them . . . the bareness of it indicated not only poverty, but a certain hopelessness.

"Kakichi?" his father inquired, his eyes narrowing. Then, suspiciously, "Is there anything wrong?" And not waiting for an answer, he called loudly for his wife. Kakichi put his bundle of clothes down in a corner.

Kakichi's mother came down the narrow stairs instantly. She was followed by his younger brother, Taiji, the hunchback, who was now sixteen years old; and after him came Yuriko, his sister, who was eleven. The children stared at their brother, their great eyes dark in their thin, pinched

faces. They scarcely remembered him and he could think
of nothing to say. But his mother put out her hands to
touch him and reproved them, saying, "Say 'welcome home'
to your brother," and they obeyed, their eyes on his face.
He felt a stranger among them, but his mother was speaking, breaking down his feeling of strangeness. "How good
to have you back, Kakichi! And you must have hot water at
once to bathe your feet," she said happily, bringing the
kettle from the stove and pouring the hot water into an
old tub, as was customary to do for one who had been on a
long journey. He was too tired to do more than obey; when
he had washed them she brought him a pair of wooden
sandals from the corner of the kitchen and watched as he
put them on. But his father, Kokichi, only glared at him
from the dim corner of the kitchen and repeated sullenly:
"Is there anything wrong that you have come home without
telling us that you were coming?"

"No. Nothing," Kakichi managed to say, uncomfortably
aware of the eyes turned upon him, and he looked towards
his mother who was getting him a cup of hot tea.

"You must be tired," her voice interrupted her husband.
"You have walked far to come home to us." And then for
the first time he saw how old and tired her face was, how
weary and faded her eyes. Their weariness smote him as
with quick pain. But the love in them, and her joy at his
coming, was like a light that suddenly lifted his heart into
a mute gladness. She came towards him, her thin figure
arching above him as he sat down on a low stool to drink
the hot tea. How good it tasted!

"You must rest, now," she told him. "You must get a
good night's sleep." Her words were so gentle . . . and it
was so long since he had known gentleness . . . that they
flowed over his weariness like a balm. He could have wept,

as a child weeps. He rose and turned to go up the stairs, and as he mounted the first step he heard his father's voice raised angrily.

"Have you no thought for me? I shall need another pint of wine, Masa. Give Yuriko some money that she may go out to buy some." Kakichi's ears caught his mother's worried remonstrance.

"But it is late. And there is no money. You must be satisfied with what you have to-night."

"And I say you shall go out and buy some," the man repeated angrily, and Kakichi turned on the stairs to see his father's hot, flushed face distorted with his displeasure. The angry man stripped off his padded kimono and, rolling it up, flung it down in front of his wife. "Go and pawn this, then," he shouted at her. Yuriko and Taiji had drawn back into a corner.

Kakichi reached down into his own pocket and drew out a small coin which he handed down to his mother. She lifted her troubled eyes to his face, made a silent gesture of dissent, but he pressed the money into her hand.

It was quiet then, and Kakichi went to his room, and to the bed that Taiji, following after, said he was to share with him. But even though he was dreadfully weary, he could not sleep. The stillness of the night was broken by the sound of the brook. It made a noise like the soft rush of falling rain. The rumble of the passing horse carts, as their wheels scraped in the ruts of the road, gradually died away. Far off he could hear the barking of a dog, chained up somewhere in the night. Everything was wrapped in the stillness of the clear mountain air.

He did not like to turn over in bed for fear of waking Taiji . . . Taiji with his poor, twisted back. It had been so long since he had thought of the child at all . . .

The quilt was not large enough to cover them both. He was cold, and shivered in the dark. He was frightened, too, at the possible consequences that might follow when his theft was discovered. Even now, as he lay here in the darkness, there might be policemen coming to get him. In and out among his thoughts upon the futility of his life in a world that seemed woefully wrong ran his memory of the face of the girl in the shop at Toyohashi. He turned restlessly.

He heard a clock strike one, and a dog far away began to bark, and a bicycle passed along the road. Taiji moved restlessly in his sleep, murmuring, and from the next room there came the sound of his mother's and father's heavy breathing. A faint light from the street-lamp dimly illuminated the room and Kakichi saw the ragged curtains which hung at the windows, and the rough, broken patches of plaster on the walls. Small wonder that two of his sisters had left their home, however shameful the occupations to which they had gone. His own shack had been no worse than this.

The clock struck three. No better things would ever come to him, probably. He had neither a job nor any money. It was all very hopeless, indeed.

Four o'clock. Three or four early horse carts from the mountains came rumbling by. A horse neighed and a cock crowed lustily. In the depths of the valley innumerable forest birds chirped sleepily. It was dawn. He fell suddenly into a deep but troubled sleep, from which he was awakened by the voice of his mother calling his name urgently. He sat up, quickly, frightened. They had come to get him!

"Kakichi . . . go quickly and call the doctor. Your father . . ."

He got to his feet, hastily pulling on the clothes he had

worn on the previous day. "He cannot move; half his body is numb. Go quickly, Kakichi." She gave him an address and he hurried away, down the quiet street to the house of the doctor. How fresh and clean and sweet everything smelled in the dawn!

The doctor was asleep, but he managed to rouse him, having time while he waited to compare his own dark dwelling with the well-lighted entrance of the dispensary. Its exterior was of Western style as was the Post Office opposite. These buildings had, he reflected, an air of cleanness and light about them. On one corner was the old dilapidated green-grocery where he used to play as a little boy, not changed at all. The cleanliness of these modern buildings stood out in marked contrast to his own poor house with its litter of rubbish thrown about the doors and out into the street. With so much dirt around, he thought, it was small wonder his father's store did not prosper.

When the doctor had dressed hastily and they had hurried back to the house, it was to find both Yuriko and Taiji crying in the hall, and his mother, Masa, her eyes dull with grief and worry, sitting beside the man on the bed. "He cannot even raise his hand," she mourned. "What shall we do?" And she wiped away the tears from her eyes with the edge of her wide sleeve. But Kakichi's eyes were on the doctor as he bent over his father, examining him. How gently he touched him!

"Is there one of Hansobo's charms in the house?" his mother asked. Hansobo was always invoked for the healing of disease. "Yuriko, see if there is not a charm of Hansobo on the god-shelf, downstairs." The little girl hurried downstairs, returning with a small, snow-white charm, which she held high in her hands, as if it were very precious. The doctor stood aside for a moment, impatiently, as Yuriko, with her hair hanging about her tearstained face, knelt by her father's pillow and rubbed the charm slowly along his arm while her mother repeated an incantation in a low voice. But no miracle happened. Kakichi's eyes sought the doctor's.

"It is a case of paralysis," the doctor said gently, and with a courtliness that, accompanied as it was by kindness, impressed Kakichi as being enviable. It might be entirely possible, he reflected, even if one could not be a good man, to be a kind one.

And when the doctor had gone and his mother had left the room to see about preparing breakfast, and Yuriko was going about the house opening all the shutters to the bright morning sunlight, he took the white charm in his hands and, very gently, rubbed the arm of the man who lay with his eyes closed on the bed, all his anger vanished. His face was drawn and old with pain.

He had no great faith in this charm. Perhaps he had no great faith in anything. The telegram that he had used as a ruse to escape from his own punishment was true enough now. He was tied to the village, to this house. He would have to find work and without much delay, but where, he had not an idea.

At breakfast he told his mother of his decision and saw her thin face flush with pleasure. "Oh, there will surely be something for you, I know," she said hopefully. Well, there were sandals to be made, he decided, seeing how badly they all stood in need of them, and taking a few coins from his meager supply, he sent Taiji out for some straw. It was a beautiful day. The sun shone so brightly and the little brook glittered like silver. The deep thick woods beyond were lovely and cool in their luxuriant greenness. He breathed in the air deeply, gratefully, as he got a round

stone out of the bed of the brook to use for a table. All
through the morning he sat in the doorway and braided
straw for sandals, looking anxiously up and down the street
occasionally to see whether the blue uniform of a policeman
might be in sight. But no one came.

He fashioned some sandals first for his mother. She
seemed to need them more than the rest. "It's a good thing
to have children," she said to him, smiling, when he had
finished them. He was curiously happy, although not without a definite apprehension as to what would happen. He
had grown up among a crowd of rough men, in which each
man looked after his own interests first. He had scarcely
known that to bring happiness to others brings it, as well,
to one's self; this was a discovery in truth, something out of
another world.

But the day was not without further trouble. For Taiji,
in attempting to light the sacred lights on the god-shelf for
his mother, slipped from the high stool and fell, injuring
his spine. He screamed for a moment and then fainted, and
for the second time that day Dr. Kurino had to be summoned. The neighbors came too, loud in their lamentations
at the misfortune that had come to the house. Yuriko, her
little face very pale, said, "Oh Taiji, Taiji," in childish
reiteration of despair at her brother's injury. Kakichi stood
by, helpless. The child must lie absolutely quiet for a long
time, the doctor ordered. He could tell nothing, yet. Masa
cried silently and Kakichi wished desperately that he could
think of some words of comfort, but he could find none.
The baker's wife came and the man who kept the wineshop, the latter very much distressed to hear of Kokichi's
indisposition, and much surprised at the appearance of
Kakichi.

"So *you* have come home! And grown tall, too," the wine-keeper greeted him. "That will mean more rice," he added morosely, but Kakichi said nothing. He was attempting to pour some water between the unconscious boy's lips.

"It is wine that he needs," the wine merchant advised, watching him doubtfully. "There's nothing better than grape wine." But the mother reached for the Hansobo charm on the god-shelf.

That charm, however, brought no added fortune to the little house. When, the following week, a telegram came to them informing them that Asa, the sister who had been sold as a dancing-girl, had run away from her owner and he demanded immediate knowledge of her whereabouts if they were known, Masa could do no more than shake her head sadly at the plight of her household.

"It is a punishment of the gods," she mourned bitterly. "We have been too poor to tend to the graves of our ancestors, and they have sent this upon us."

But Kakichi, while he could say nothing to refute her, did not believe her. In his heart he knew only too well that it was his home-coming that had brought these tribulations upon his household . . . his home-coming as a liar and a thief. It could not be anything but that.

CHAPTER III

A KINDLY NEIGHBOR

IT WAS EVIDENT THEN, AND MADE INCREASINGLY SO IN THE days that followed, that the family's financial situation was desperate. Making sandals would not afford them a living. What they earned in the shop was inadequate to meet their needs, and there was no money to put into the purchasing of new stock, with the result that both the stock and the customers decreased day by day. Masa, troubled and anxious, and worn out with her care of the two invalids and her attempt to find enough for them all to eat, was forgetful, and made all sorts of blunders in the shop. She worried, too, because it was December, and, as she reminded Kakichi, there would be no rice paste for the New Year, no offering to make to the gods. She went wearily, but faithfully, to the temple each day with prayers for her husband and Taiji, but Kakichi placed but meager faith in her going. He went out seeking a job. It was one of the most difficult things he had ever done, and he was sick with discouragement, but just when things seemed the most hopeless he found one. It was at a water mill, belonging to Mata, the miller. The wages were small, it was true, and the job temporary, only lasting until the New Year; but he was hungry, and it was with real gratitude in his heart that he began his work.

The work was easier than he had expected; his duties were to measure out the unhulled rice from the straw sacks and pour it into the motor, and then pack the cleaned and whitened rice into bags again.

As he drew near to the millhouse, one December morning, he noticed that several strange dogs were lying outside. He opened the door, and, to his surprise, found a man inside. He was fast asleep on a piece of straw matting which was spread on the earthen floor of the hut. In his arms was a monkey, asleep, and behind him and around him were dogs, large and small, keeping him warm. Counting those outside, there were nine of them. He lifted his head as Kakichi entered, smiled sleepily and nodded.

"Good morning."

"You shouldn't be sleeping here," remonstrated Kakichi, irritably; adding, "on the earth."

The man made no reply, only reached out a hand and with a gesture that was strangely like a caress laid his hand on the earthen floor. Kakichi scrutinized his face closely. He had a beard and his skin was fair, his forehead broad, and his eyes clear and bright. There was about his face and expression something—Kakichi sought in his mind for a word to express it—something fine. He was probably a hermit; they were not uncommon in the hills. He had on several laborer's coats one over the other, and over that a tight-sleeved kimono. The monkey was sleeping in his arms as though he felt perfectly safe. The nine dogs were of all sizes and kinds. The largest one was a fox-hound. There was one as big as a calf, who was crouching behind his master's back, and growled when he saw Kakichi come in. There was one coal-black dog, something like a pointer, who was lying near his master's feet. There was a spotted dog and two setters, who, with outstretched paws, like the dog images of the temples, were guarding him. A brown dog lay near his pillow, a white dog beside him, and in the corner a bulldog was curled into a ball. Two smaller dogs were chasing each other around the mortar of the mill. There was something humorous about it and Kakichi grinned in more friendly fashion.

Something in the natural repose of the man and all the dogs made him feel ashamed for having spoken so curtly. He turned to go about his work, emptying rice into the mortar and connecting it up with the water wheel so that the clatter of the mill began once again. The sun had not yet risen. Great cedars and beech trees loomed out of the early morning mist which enveloped the plateau like a veil of transparent beauty. The spears of frosted grass, glistening like crystals, lifted themselves above the earth, reflecting the pale morning light. Kakichi went on sifting the rice and collecting in a sieve the grains which clung to the straw. It would be another hour before the owner appeared.

The hermit got up, and with the monkey perched on his shoulder went out to wash himself in the stream. Kakichi watched curiously from the open door. Here was no ordinary beggar, such as one often saw seeking lodging for the night in the lumber camps. The nine dogs followed him. They scampered through the water and all about in the brush with an evident delight. When the man had wiped his face on a towel he faced the east, and although Kakichi could not see his face, there was something in the attitude of the man, something that suggested the fact that he was worshiping. The monkey still clung to his back. He would leave now, Kakichi thought, but the man came back into the house.

"Beautiful day!" he addressed Kakichi again. Kakichi made no reply. When one was seriously occupied with the business of earning enough food for the day, it was of small account how the day was.

The hermit turned his face towards the hills beyond the stream, bare hills, barren of all save scraggly brush and twisted pines.

"Beautiful country," he added, and to this Kakichi grunted his dissent. Beautiful! That hillside! The man was an idiot. He glanced at his rapt face, and the man laughed.

"Ah, that is my fault," he apologized gently. "You see I see it as it might be," he said enigmatically. But Kakichi had an unwarranted desire to speak further with this man.

"Isn't it cold, sleeping on the ground that way?"

"Why, no! Not at all! It's a lot warmer to sleep with my dogs than to sleep under bedclothes." The monkey stared at Kakichi with small piercing bright eyes from the man's shoulder.

"Do you always sleep on the roadside like this? Have you no home?" the boy pursued.

"Oh, yes. I've a home, but I'm fond of these mountains, you see, so I wander about like this, with my monkey and my dogs."

"And you're really not cold?" Kakichi persisted. The man laughed, showing his fine white teeth.

"Why not try it and see? It's really very comfortable . . . and comforting, too."

Kakichi thought of his own home, and the thin quilts, and their insufficient width, then looked at the dogs. "Well, it might be a good idea," he agreed.

"They're really invaluable," the man continued. "Sometimes, you know, you meet wolves and bears in the mountains, but you are always quite safe if you have dogs along. The smallest one is the strongest. They do not correct you or make any suggestions, and they eat scraps of any kind of food. They're really no trouble. But what about you?" he asked suddenly, kindly, his brown eyes holding a friendly interest. "Do you work here all alone? Why not let me help you? You see, that's one of the virtues of my life; I have all the time there is. If you'd let me help you for a half day or a whole day, I'd be glad to."

Kakichi was somewhat astonished at the man's friendliness. There was a kind of magnetism about this man. He wanted to know more about him. He wanted—which was even stranger—he wanted to talk to him. "I thank you," he said, stiffly, "but there's no need for you to help."

The hermit placed the bag of rice which he had used as a pillow back on the pile again, and swept the room clean with a broom, even to brushing up the road in front of the millhouse. He then went into the thicket, and breaking off some dry branches, built a fire outside on the ground. On this he placed an enamel cup and a cooking utensil from his willow basket and began preparations for what would apparently be a very simple breakfast.

Kakichi regarded him from the doorway, and finally called out to him, "You have everything that you need?" And the man said quietly, looking all about him, up at the hills and then back to the fire at his feet, "Yes, thank you. I have everything."

Kakichi was somewhat astonished at the man's friendli-thing he needed, he thought, feeling the quietness of the man enter into him with the words.

In the days that approached the New Year, Kakichi worked steadily. At home he helped in the shop, attempting to put things into order. The burden of caring for his father and Taiji fell mostly upon his mother, and her anxiety deepened. Kokichi was no better; even in his dire illness his impatience and bad temper oppressed them all. Taiji showed no improvement, and despite Dr. Kurino's statement that in a case of this kind they needed both time and patience, Masa was insistent in her belief that her failure to placate the gods had caused their misfortune. And now, with the New Year and its customary offering to the gods rendered impossible through their dire circumstances, her spirits were indeed low.

Ah, if only he had not taken that money! was Kakichi's one wish. It was so little, but it would have been a sum sufficient to buy rice paste for his mother. It was so little, but he had run away from the payment of it, yet not, strangely enough, from the existence of the debt itself. Nothing would be righted until it was paid, he believed.

On the last day of the year they were awakened early in the morning by the sound of their neighbors, the blacksmith and his wife, vigorously pounding their rice. A short time later Kakichi's mother called to him from downstairs. Yuki, the blacksmith's wife, had come to their door.

"Our steaming baskets are all hot for the rice. Why not come over and join us? We have more rice than we need."

His mother hesitated. "It was for the god-shelf that I wanted it," she told her young neighbor.

"Well, there is still plenty, whatever your need. Let Kakichi come."

Kakichi followed her across the narrow yard to her house, marveling the while at this unexpected kindness. Yuki was only twenty-five, but even his short stay in the village had shown her to be unlike most of the women of her age. She had a charm and friendliness, an openness of manner that distinguished her from the rest. His mother had told him that she played a leading part in the village woman's association, and she had lately been going to a teacher of Christianity who lived in the lower village. His name was Murano, and beyond the fact that he was a Christian Masa knew nothing of him. She did not approve of him and the reasons she gave Kakichi were simple enough. "If you become a Christian, you have to give up the worship of your ancestors and then it is impossible to be respected by your neighbors. And, moreover, your ancestors will surely send punishment upon you."

But Kakichi saw no evidence of any such effect in the orderly, happy household into which he entered that morning. He felt, too, that Christianity could not be such a bad religion if it taught one to proffer help, even before it was asked.

Her husband, Totaro, and three young apprentices were mixing the rice paste. They welcomed Kakichi warmly.

"It is nice to have you, Kakichi," Totaro said kindly, noting the boy's shyness and hesitancy. "With your father and brother ill, you must find things very difficult. We have spoken of how fortunate it is that you should be home."

Fortunate! Kakichi looked at him.

"Come ahead; the fire's just right for steaming."

The apprentices were singing as they worked, and obviously enjoying it. Yuki gave him a mallet and a wooden pail. He watched them as they formed the rice paste into balls, and followed their movements. He enjoyed it, and hesitantly, still unsurely, he joined in their singing. Through the shining windows of the bright, warm little kitchen he saw the snow falling far off on the mountains, gray against the gray sky.

"Ah, now that our neighbor has come, we make real progress," Totaro observed, and Kakichi felt warmed at the words. The word "neighbor" had a new meaning. The kitchen became a lively place. Yuki went from one to another giving each an ample supply of rice flour, and piling up the red trays with the cakes.

Then suddenly one of the apprentices spoke of the

hermit. "Who is this man with the dogs and the monkey, who lives in a lodginghouse at the edge of the village? Some say he goes about to the sick, when he is asked, and that they are better for seeing him." Kakichi raised his head quickly to listen.

Totaro nodded. "I've seen him; a most unusual fellow. I have heard that if he is offered money he won't take it, but instead he asks for some scraps to give to his dogs, or some rice for his monkey. He never asks for anything for himself."

"I'd like to be able to go through life as easily as that," interposed one of the apprentices.

"As a hermit? Sleeping wherever he finds a place to sleep?" inquired another doubtfully.

"There's something enviable about it," Totaro suggested; "the ease of it."

Kakichi lifted up his voice to agree.

"But I think," Totaro went on, "that he must be ill. I have not seen him about lately." Kakichi felt troubled at this information. However invaluable the dogs might be, they could be of little use to him if he were ill. The extreme gentleness of the man's face came to his mind. Perhaps he needed a neighbor.

The rice for Kakichi's household, being a small amount, was finished in a very short time. Kakichi thanked the young couple warmly, and then started off for his work at the mill, leaving his mother, who had joined them, to carry home the small tray of cakes. When he returned that evening he found the rice cakes in their place on the god-shelf. She smiled at him, happily.

"Perhaps now the New Year may be brighter for us, Kakichi. Luckier. Happier." He looked down into her face. Strangely enough it seemed so to him, too. It was a time of the year too when the people in the Eastern world made what they called resolutions. He had a dim wish that he might be kindly, gracious, neighborly; it was just possible that his mother's gods might recognize that wish. But they seemed, those gods, impersonal and afar.

"Mother," he said suddenly, impulsively, his face brightening. "Could I take a few of these rice cakes to a hermit in the village who is ill? He may need food."

Something in the brightness of his face arrested her refusal. "Yes. Take some, of course, Kakichi."

With a new eagerness and joy he finished his own simple supper of rice mixed with wheat, wrapped some of the cakes in paper and started out for the lodginghouse at the edge of the village. It was a small, bare room, and the hermit lay on a wooden bed in the corner, the dogs lying disconsolately about him on the floor. Kakichi proffered the cakes shyly, and the man's gratitude and pleasure were clearly evident. But he pulled up the thin quilts about his chest and spoke reassuringly when Kakichi asked to be of more help. His brown eyes smiled.

"This was all I needed for to-day and, see, you have brought it," he told him. "I shall be up to-morrow, you shall see, and in a few days I'll be fit again. You are a kindly young man," he told him, and he laid one hand on the silky head of the dog sitting nearest the bed.

A young man! Yes, he was, Kakichi thought suddenly. A man, and not a boy any longer. The thought was new, and a bit frightening.

CHAPTER IV

A HEAVENLY GUIDE

THE DAY'S EXPERIENCES WERE NOT AT AN END. KAKICHI walked home slowly, somewhat reluctant to go back to its illness and confusion. He was tired, and his thoughts had turned, for the first time in days, to the girl in Toyohashi. There was little for a young man to do in this town by way of entertainment. And then suddenly a woman's voice addressed him, pleasantly: "Good evening!"

He stopped abruptly. It was their neighbor, Yuki, and she was about to enter the door of what had once been a draper's shop. A rectangle of yellow lamplight fell across the walk at her feet from the window.

"Good evening," he returned politely, wondering why she was out alone. Through the window he caught a glimpse of some wooden benches and an organ, with three or four young people gathered near it and a man talking to them. This must be the place where Mr. Murano held his Christian meetings, Kakichi decided, and was about to pass on when a young man and a girl, also about to enter the shop, paused and Yuki introduced them. The girl's name was Hana and she worked in the Post Office. The young man he did not remember as ever having seen before.

"It's nice to have a newcomer," said the girl cordially, addressing Kakichi. They thought he was coming along. He glanced again through the windows. Well, after Yuki's kindness of the morning, he supposed that he could do nothing else. Moreover, one visit surely would do no harm; he was curious. So he entered with them, although somewhat uncomfortably.

The room was warm in the lamplight and there was about its occupants that same air of friendliness that Yuki had demonstrated. Mr. Murano was tall and slender, his thick dark hair slightly gray at the temples. His face was somehow reminiscent of the hermit's, although Kakichi could not have told why he thought so.

He had lived in Lower Tsugu all his life, and there was no one in the village who did not know him, for he had formerly been a teacher in the primary school and likewise had had a small private school where he taught the Chinese and Japanese classics to private pupils. He was related by marriage to Dr. Kurino, and was braving the criticism of the villages in teaching Christianity.

Kakichi looked about him curiously. When he was a boy he remembered this room as having been piled with boxes and bundles wrapped in straw matting. It had been cleaned and repaired, and despite its bareness there was about it a difference that Kakichi could not define. It held *something*.

Yuki took her place at the organ and they sang a short hymn together. He knew neither the words nor the music, so he could do no more than listen. Their voices were soft and low, soothing when one was tired.

Then Mr. Murano read, from the Bible. No one had ever read to Kakichi. Certainly he had never been read to from the Bible. He listened, not understanding much of it, but becoming more and more aware of the strange beauty of the words and of a rare listening quality in those few people about him. Their faces were lifted, and alight; they heard and understood. These were words they believed. He could not yet understand, perhaps, and without knowledge how could one believe? But the sincerity and humility of the words could not be mistaken, and these were qualities which, despite difference in speech or mode of expression, were communicable. In the dimly lighted room Kakichi began to feel relaxed and at peace.

This man was different from the fortuneteller. He, too, might know all about one . . . but with a difference. Kakichi could tell *him* about his thieving, feeling that in the mere telling some of the burden would be lost.

One sentence, repeated twice, caught his attention and his imagination fastened upon it curiously: "Blessed are the pure in heart, for they shall see God." He said that where there was clarity there was vision; through clear and shining panes of glass light could shine with undiminished brightness. Kakichi could understand that. But this God of whom he spoke so tenderly, with such understanding? And the man Jesus? Ah, here was much to learn.

In this teaching, Mr. Murano said, one cultivated the spirit, lifting one's life, as one's prayers, with confidence and perfect trust.

Certain scenes flashed unaccountably through Kakichi's mind as he listened, more intently now: a flight of cranes above the blue waters of the river, the snowy mountaintops veiled in the soft mists of dawn. All his memories of sunlight on the clear waters of the Toyo River, and of the serenity of the twilight hours . . . things he had noted, yet never in the way he noted them all now in memory, crowded in upon him, harmonizing and blending with the spirit of those in that small, quiet room, and communicating to him a hitherto unexperienced bliss. This quietude, this reverence, these beauties only now perceived were linked in his mind with the God of whom Mr. Murano spoke . . . "the one and only God in Heaven." It was a God of whom he would like to learn. Mr. Murano spoke of serving the Lord with a new heart in the coming year. He spoke of temptations to be overcome through right effort and prayer. And then he prayed.

Kakichi bowed his head as he saw the others do, and in his heart he voiced his first prayer, for this new heart Mr. Murano spoke of, for a purity sufficient so that he, too, might see. It was not lacking in sincerity; the very uttering of it lifted him higher than he had ever before been lifted.

Standing with them all, before they departed, some of his hesitancy disappeared. He attempted to join their conversation, gratefully aware of their friendliness. Both Yuki and the girl Hana were different from the woman he had known at the lumber camp. Yuki was lovely and kind; she was beautiful, not only his neighbor but his friend. They walked home together and, hesitantly, he said that he would like to come again if he might.

"Of course," she told him warmly. "Of course, you may come." And he felt as though he had known them all for a long time, and not just for a few hours of his life. He felt—how could he define it?—at home! Comforted! Fed!

CHAPTER V

THE HERMIT AND THE SECRETS OF THE MOUNTAIN

ON THE MORNING OF NEW YEAR'S DAY, HIS MOTHER ROSE early to light the lights on the god-shelf, and to visit the shrines of many gods to petition them for good fortune in the coming days. Kakichi performed his services in the kitchen, where, more and more, and to his surprise, he found himself able to be of service. There was soup to be prepared before his mother returned, and he had had enough experience in the logging camps to know how to do that.

Before his mother returned there was a knock on the door, and he found there, to his astonishment, the hermit with his dogs and his monkey. He had a small drum strapped to his back.

"A happy New Year to you, young man. How would you like to earn a little money to-day? I'm going up to some of the villages in the mountains, and you can beat the drum while the monkey dances. He makes the children laugh; you shall see. Will you come?"

Kakichi looked helplessly from the man's smiling face to the monkey's bright, knowing eyes.

"But I can't beat a drum," he protested.

"Oh, I shall teach you," urged the hermit. "I might even teach you to plant trees."

Kakichi laughed. "To plant trees?" he echoed in amusement. "I've never done that, either; but I know how to cut

33

them down. I'd be of no use to you, I'm afraid," he added, but not without some regret, because the prospect of a day with this man interested him tremendously.

"On the contrary, you would be of great use. I live alone a great deal, you see, and it is good to have someone to talk to."

Kakichi still hesitated. "I would have to wait for my mother to return, first," he suggested. "Why not come in and have some soup with us, while we wait?"

The hermit came in, and Masa returned almost at once. Yuriko was summoned and they sat around the warm kitchen, eating the soup and some rice cakes. The monkey, with whom Yuriko was childishly delighted, squeezed in between them gratefully, warming himself at the fire.

Kakichi was anxious to go; he felt that even though he had lived in the mountains, this man possessed an intimate knowledge and love of them that he lacked. A holiday in the village, moreover, did not attract him greatly. So he borrowed a coat of his father's, wishing that he might have had one of his own, and, with the drum on his shoulder, he followed along after the hermit over the narrow, winding, frosted path that wound upwards, through the mountains. The flags flew from the roofs of the village houses, the red suns on the white fields bright in the sun. It was a beautiful day.

The dogs trotted along beside them, some ahead, some behind, and the monkey blinked from the hermit's broad shoulder. The hermit turned his head to look back at Kakichi as they jogged easily along.

"You know, these mountains were once at the bottom of the sea," he told him. "Over half of the land of Japan has been lifted out of the sea. That's why you find these broad plateaus on top of the mountains, and fossils with shells in them in the rocks of the streams. Did you know that?"

No, he had not known; he listened eagerly.

"I believe, you know, that if Japan does not cultivate these lands that have been lifted up for her use, if she lets her land, or her people, lie fallow, the sea will one day swallow them up again."

"But these mountains," protested Kakichi, looking about him at the vast stretches of wilderness.

"Are not fit for use? Because they are not used. That is a law. There are ten million acres of mountain land here that might be placed under cultivation. It is because Japan grows nothing but rice that she does not prosper. Since she is a land of mountains and sea, she would have no trouble with her food supply if she would resolve to eat these things which the mountains and the sea afford. There are all sorts of things to eat that come from the mountains . . . there are many more that could and should be grown here. As long as a man has proteids, starches, and fats . . . that is, some kind of oil . . . these three . . . he can live. Better use could be made of the chestnuts and acorns; we ought to cultivate chestnuts. Our ancestors did. There's more nourishment in chestnuts than in rice, and Japan is a country where chestnuts grow well. How would it be, Kakichi, if we were to plant a few trees? Oh, but I forgot; you said that you had been taught only to cut them down." He smiled at the boy.

"That is true. I learned that well."

"It's not difficult to learn how to make them grow; you must have faith. The trouble is that people only know how to cut them down; they must be re-educated. A chestnut tree matures in four years. And one chestnut tree will bear one bushel of nuts in a season. As you can plant about one hundred and sixty trees to an acre, that makes one hundred and sixty bushels, and that means that you get a better income than from the twenty bushels of rice which the same amount of land will produce."

Kakichi's eyes widened at these calculations. "But," he suggested, "if you could not find the people who would eat the chestnuts . . . as they will eat the rice?"

"The idea then is to use them to feed to the pigs. You feed pigs on chestnuts, and then you eat the pigs."

Kakichi laughed heartily. "You have thought that out well," he commended; then on a sudden impulse he asked: "How have you come to know all these things? What is your name?" The hermit stepped to whistle to one of his dogs.

"In reality I know very little. My name? Folks call me Kakube-e, the monkey-man. Another name I have is 'God's child,' a wanderer over the face of the earth." He laughed with a lighthearted laugh, as though this was the name that he liked best to have, and this occupation of wandering the one most to be cherished. Kakichi was anxious to hear more about him but he seemed in no hurry to talk of himself.

"What do you say, Kakichi?" he suggested at length. "Shall we stop at the village of Neba to-night?"

"Neba? But that's very near, isn't it? We can easily reach it by noon."

"Yes, we can, of course. But it is a nice place to stay overnight. There is a good inn there."

"You take life easy," Kakichi told him enviously.

"Yes, I take things easy. To take them otherwise only makes everything very difficult. It seems more human to me not to make a penny or lose it, than to make a million and lose a million and a half."

"That sounds reasonable," Kakichi agreed, wondering

why he had never met anyone before in his life who could talk in this fashion.

"Well, I'm putting this reasonable idea into practice." He stopped for a minute and gazed at the still woods all about them. "There is a great virtue in that, Kakichi; a great lesson for you who are young . . . putting truths into practice." Kakichi's eyes rested on the man's quiet face. So many countless new thoughts had been formulating within him these past weeks, breaking slowly through the long-accustomed reticence of years, and there was no hesitancy now in his desire to speak. But there was, too, no need. He nodded, agreeing, and looked up at the great branches of the oak trees, etched in black against the clear blue of the sky. They went along towards the village of Neba.

"Kakube-e," Kakichi said suddenly, "what do you mean when you say you are God's child?"

The man's reply was brief. "The whole universe is full of God. God dwells in our hearts, in our wisdom, in our will, our whole life. That is why we are children of God. It's something to be very grateful for, I think. An inheritance to use."

There was a pause and then the boy pursued: "Is this part of the teaching of Jesus, Kakube-e?"

"Yes."

"This Christianity . . . it is a good religion, then?" he went on eagerly, awaiting the answer.

"It's a good religion. It's a religion that appeals to the people of the whole world. There can be nothing wrong about it, for it teaches the love of God and the love of man. It is based on love. God means love. I add to it the love of the land. There is much in that thought . . . it includes love of growth, of productivity, of usefulness."

Kakichi said: "Yes? Go on, Kakube-e."

"The Founder of Christianity, Jesus, was a wonderful man. I think the most significant thing about him was that he was a carpenter. We all ought to be carpenters like he was. Even though one just handles trees, one ought to be like him. One makes many mistakes in one's youth that cannot be retrieved," he added wistfully, "but I wish I might have been a carpenter."

The two of them walked the next mile or two in silence. To-day, no horse-drawn cart passed them, nor did they see anyone; nothing but their purple shadows cast by the sun on the yellow sand of the road.

When they reached Neba, Kakube-e showed Kakichi how to beat the drum. After ten minutes of hard work the little drum responded to his touch.

"That's it," encouraged Kakube-e. "If you keep the rhythm, the monkey can dance. He's really quite stupid, but he recognizes rhythm; it's that that is important. It's important in life too," he added reflectively.

It was a strange vocation for him to have chosen, Kakichi thought with amusement . . . beating a drum for a monkey. For a moment he hoped there would be no one here who would recognize him, but he forgot this quite soon in watching the very apparent delight of the adults and children who gathered in a circle about them when the sound of the drum, re-echoing among the huge cedar trees of the grove at the edge of the village, attracted them.

The monkey jumped down from Kakube-e's shoulder, began his comic dance, never for a moment unmindful of the rope around his neck, or of the pennies or bits of food thrown down to him. The pennies he immediately brought to his master, but the food was his own and he consumed it with evident relish. A crow perched on the tip of a branch cawed loudly, as if in approval, and the nine dogs chased around the edge of the grove, enjoying themselves hugely. Kakube-e sang, repeating the one short verse until the children knew it and joined their voices with his, and begged him to sing again. Kakichi laughed aloud at the infectious joy of them, reflecting what a long while it had been since he had laughed like that.

"You see, Kakichi," the hermit told him, "they think that if a 'monkey-man' doesn't come round at the New Year, they won't have good luck the whole year through. So it's really social service work that we are doing," he added, laughing.

For three days they wandered in the mountains, stopping for a half day at a town where a co-operative silk industry was flourishing, and where the village girls who worked in the mills and the industry's managers shared profit and loss in common, with great success. Kakube-e discoursed at length upon the advisability of some such form of organization as this in the society of the future. When Kakichi actually saw the place with his own eyes, and what was being done there, strange as it all was to him, and new, he was ashamed of the restricted life he had led, of his ignorance, and the narrow ideas that his life had afforded him.

Kakube-e showed him, too, a cave on a mountain pass where he had spent one winter. The dishes and a tin box were still there, just as he had left them, and the inside of the cave had not been disturbed at all. It was set in a thick grove of fir and boxwood trees, very near a valley; and its floor, which was about six feet by three, had been leveled off neatly. There was a cookstove, too, some old magazines which had evidently been much read, and ten or more pieces of firewood, neatly split and piled up at the back of the cave.

"It's two miles and a half to the nearest house," said Kakube-e. "Of course it's lonely, but it has great advantages. You don't hear anything about the disagreeable happenings of the world outside. Your heart becomes as clear as the mountain stream. I'm coming back here after this summer. Last winter it was so lovely here that I stayed until the spring. If human beings learned how to live simply, Kakichi, and would not be led astray by material things, this would be quite a different world in which to live. They do not know how to be still, and hear."

Kakichi began suddenly to see the reason why this man was different.

"But had you no business in which you were engaged, Kakube-e?"

"Oh, yes. I was a shipbuilder in Osaka, years ago. At the time of the war I had docks eight or nine hundred feet long. I was very prosperous. I had money . . . a home . . . a wife. I was a success. But all that I did was for myself . . . never for others. So I lost all that I had. And came to wander here, in the mountains, so that I could get that which I had never had." As he talked he stroked the little monkey sitting on his knee.

"I know," he continued gently, "that it would seem that you have nothing. There is your father sick, and your brother injured. And you have no work. But you will see, if you think for a moment, that you really have a great deal. Youth . . . a steady mind with which to learn. A chance to right these wrong things in your home. A mother."

Kakichi was silent. The sun had sunk low in the west and golden clouds overspread the sky above the hills like a great fan. A narrow brook babbled as it flowed in a valley about three or four hundred feet below the cave, and far in the distance the smoke from the houses in the village rose in the clear air.

"I must see," he determined, "that there is a column of smoke rising from the chimney of my poor house, even though it is only a thin thread of smoke. If I can have the patience and steadiness and wisdom of this man, I can do anything." And he decided that now he must return to his mother; surely she needed him, and he had been away for three days. He resisted Kakube-e's suggestion that he start home in the morning; there was upon him an urgency to be at home this night and he knew the way well. So, bidding farewell to the hermit, and attempting to tell him how much these days had meant to him, he hurried along the curving, twisting mountain path. As he descended it grew quite dark, but even the darkness was changed. Fear had gone from him, and all sense of loneliness. He, too, was a child of God, just as Kakube-e had said. Those words had sunk down into the very core of his being, and had deeply impressed him. They linked him up, too, he felt, with the religion of Mr. Murano. Reflecting on these things, he walked through the darkness, with the road under his feet faintly luminous although hemmed in by the blackness.

It was past midnight when he reached home, but when he knocked on the door, Yuriko came quickly to open it and welcomed him lovingly, as though she had missed him.

"Oh, Kakichi . . . it is *you!*" she said happily. "Welcome home!"

His mother was already in bed, but she called to him. "Kakichi, I have good news for you. Yuki has been over and the blacksmith has kindly offered to have you as a helper in his shop, from to-morrow. Would you do that? They will give you a yen a day; it is for you to decide. It is very little, I know . . . but . . ."

Yes, it was little, he thought, but it was only because men were eager to make much that they went without work. If they were content only to have something to eat, God would, in some way or another, surely give a man that. And thinking gratefully upon these things, he fell into a deep slumber.

CHAPTER VI

LIFE'S KALEIDOSCOPE

ALTHOUGH KAKICHI KNEW NOTHING OF THE BLACKSMITH'S trade, he found the work interesting beyond his expectations. He was thrilled to see how the iron, once it was subjected to heat, could be made to take any shape desired. There was something vaguely symbolic to him in the process. He was warmed, too, by the continued kindness of the mistress of the house. His master was a man of good sense, and kindly, too, but it was Yuki who showed countless small favors to Kakichi and to his family. Every Sunday night he accompanied her to the draper's shop to hear Mr. Murano, and Yuki had given him a Bible. But no one knew of his going. He pursued this course with growing uneasiness, recognizing clearly that he would have to acknowledge openly to his parents, and to the village people, his intention of pursuing this faith at which they, for the most part, scoffed. He wondered why this religion had not spread more quickly in Japan, and yet he, himself, was hesitant about admitting it. He would have liked to tell his parents of this precious teaching he was imbibing, although he knew his mother's opposition to it. But perhaps there was no better way of telling them than by his own conduct.

This thought thrilled him. He began immediately to put it into action. The first manifestation of it appeared to him in the growing attachment between himself and his father. The next came when, going at the urgent persuasion of

Chukichi, a young fellow who worked with him at the blacksmith's shop, to a night-life café where there was a young waitress with whom Chukichi was in love, and where he was exposed to the wiles of other waitresses, he was surprised to find how without savor these things were to him now. They presented a world different from that which he had glimpsed through the eyes of Kakube-e, or Mr. Murano. They left him only impatient to be home, where he felt that there was real work to be accomplished.

In his spare time he now undertook the new experience of reading aloud to his father. Taiji, lying shrunken and still, would turn his head from the bed opposite to listen, his large eyes fastened upon his brother's face. Kakichi read anything he could lay his hands upon, and the supply was naturally limited in so small a village. But there were the papers, and books on history and travel, and even novels. He read with growing ease and with growing knowledge. The more he gave to help others, the more he found he was receiving himself. His mother marveled at his patience and his eagerness to learn. But he at the same time was marveling at her loyalty and her industry. During his long separation from her he had not thought of her with much gratitude, but now her life made a deep impression upon him. She had much to bear, and to the very highest degree of which she was capable she was bearing it. Even her religion, poor as it now seemed to him, received her highest devotion. He would often lift his eyes from his reading to see her standing before the god-shelf, and he knew that her thoughts were upon her husband and her younger son. How he wished he could share with her his great discoveries in Jesus, but failing that, he knew that nothing he might say could comfort her.

Nevertheless, Kakichi's family of five managed to get

through the long, lonely months of the winter, though often they had nothing more than rice gruel to eat. A village credit association, of which the blacksmith's wife was a member, advanced his mother a sum sufficient to replenish the small store's depleted stock, a good fortune over which she greatly rejoiced, as did Kakichi, save for the fact that the necessity to repay his small debt to Maruhachi gave him no rest.

Late in May, when the forests were ablaze with their new foliage and the small cuckoos for which they were famous sang joyously all through the day, his mother said suddenly: "Take this money I have carefully saved and go to my home village of Gamagori. It is the third anniversary of my father's death. Someone must pay respect to the dead or a greater misfortune will surely come upon us." Kakichi saw his chance. Gamagori was but a short distance from Maruhachi's and he had just completed saving enough money to repay that which he had stolen. In a spirit of great joy and relief Kakichi started for Gamagori.

He reached the little town, on the sea's edge, quite early in the evening and went directly to the house of his mother's older brother, where his mother had insisted that he must stay. His uncle was a shipbuilder, and a man of moderate means, and his home near the shore was comfortable beyond all Kakichi's knowledge of comfort.

"Kakichi!" cried his uncle, recognizing him. "You have come just at the right time. The greatest boat race of the century is to be held day after to-morrow. You must stay and see my boat, the *Hatsue Maru*, win again. It has won two years in succession and if it wins again it will bring me the cup."

Kakichi had never seen a boat race, neither had he experienced the ease and comfort and informality with which

these relatives lived. He began to realize that here was another, brighter world than the dismal and poverty-stricken
one he had known. Oh, that he might with persistent effort bring this world into being in his own life and that of
his family's. He would gladly stay for the race, he agreed,
but first he must attend to his mother's errand and he must
visit Maruhachi's lumberyard.

As a part of doing honor to his ancestors' graves, he attended the Buddhist memorial service. Early in the morning
a group of the village saints came and chanted a prayer
from the *Book of the Law*, and the priests from the temple
recited similar prayers, all of which were quite unintelligible to Kakichi. How lacking in warmth and inspiration
they seemed when compared with the peaceful, loving teaching of Mr. Murano. Mr. Murano's God seemed nearer,
more real.

He hurried then along the Toyo River to the Maruhachi
Company. At the office he found, as usual, the cross old
clerk still writing busily in his account book. It seemed a
long time to Kakichi since he had been here, and quite a
different person who had returned. The clerk greeted him,
remarking that it had been a long time since they had seen
him.

"Yes, a long while," Kakichi agreed. "Could I see the
master? Is he in?"

"I'll call him for you," said the clerk, and he went into
the back of the building. Maruhachi came at once, and his
greeting was so cordial as to embarrass Kakichi exceedingly.
It was no easy task to broach the subject upon which
Kakichi wished to speak at once, and yet he was surprised at
the ease with which he spoke.

"When I was here last year, Maruhachi San," he began
abruptly, "I collected five yen from the boxmaker and did

not pay it to you. I have come to pay it now." And he held out the money.

Maruhachi hesitated. "I know of no such transaction, Kakichi. I shall have to ask the bookkeeper." He went into the next office and returned after a few moments, saying that the bookkeeper had no record of this debt.

"Are you sure?" he began.

"Oh, quite sure, master. Do take it, please," urged Kakichi in embarrassment. "I shall never feel right until I have repaid it." And so saying he thrust the coin into the man's hand, and hurried out into the street.

When he had reached the corner he stood quite still for a moment, breathing a brief prayer of gratitude in his heart that now, at last, this debt was paid. And as he looked up at the blue sky between the high piles of lumber on either side of him it seemed to him that the heavens were so close that, if he lifted up his hands, he might touch them.

On his return to his uncle's house, Kakichi heard the sound of women's voices, and on entering he found his aunt entertaining a group of young girls. As she had no children and was very fond of young people, this group came almost daily to see her. Kakichi would have withdrawn but she insisted that he must meet them. He found them friendly and interesting, speaking intelligently of the theater and of the coming race with an ease and total lack of embarrassment in his presence that astonished him. He had had so few opportunities to talk in a friendly way with young women outside his family that he was at first somewhat ill at ease.

"You needn't be shy," his aunt sought to relieve him. "These girls are all like daughters, and we are all great friends."

While they appeared to be only poor factory girls, he noticed that several of them had very beautiful eyes. There was about them a sweetness and naturalness that soon set him at ease. Three of them dressed their hair in modern style. They all looked at him with frank curiosity.

"Surely, here you should be able to pick out a suitable bride," his uncle teased. "Have your choice, Kakichi."

The girls laughed, and Kakichi felt his face flush. "That's not very complimentary, uncle," one of them replied. "Besides, I had planned on becoming a fisherman's wife."

"Oh no, Tama," objected another of the girls. "That's *such* a poor idea. When the winds are right, they're off to fish, and, if they don't fish, you have nothing to eat. It must be most uncomfortable . . . being married to a fisherman."

One girl, with a lovely brown skin and large dark eyes, smiled up at him sweetly.

"I think you will be quite safe," she suggested gently. "Aren't you of an age, soon, when you will be entering military service, and so escape us all?"

He nodded. His uncle addressed this girl at once. "Now, Yoshie," he remonstrated, "just when we would marry him off as our own son, you conspire against it."

But Yoshie did not answer. Her long lashes covered her eyes as she bent over some work in her lap. Kakichi noticed what beautiful hands she had, small, but with so much character in the strong fingers.

"I don't think men should be married off without their own consent," she persisted. "I wouldn't if I were a man."

Just then the cry went up from outside that the boats were being launched for the races and it was time to begin. Kakichi's uncle rose at once.

"You come with me, Kakichi. The girls can wait at the

dock here for the reports, but you must come with me and see it from beginning to end. Would you like to?"

Would he like to? Kakichi's face shone with excitement and pleasure.

There was a great deal of cheering as the big boat left the props and slid down into the water. Kakichi's aunt and the girls on the dock watched with excited interest.

"Oh, I do hope it won't end in a riot like it did last year," said Tama.

"Well," reflected Kakichi's aunt, "with our boat winning twice, there are those who are quite likely to show their envy if we win again."

The boats were darting forward like great white birds with their wide wings outspread under a sky of deep, pure amethyst.

Every boat made good speed, so that the *Pet Hawk* was third until they rounded the buoy which marked the end of the two and one-half mile course. At this point it outdistanced the others and took first place. Unfortunately, however, the man handling the helm was so clumsy in the confusion of a few seconds that they intruded slightly upon the course of the boat next to them. The *Pet Hawk* came in first at the final goal but there was a protest entered at once from the other boat. Almost immediately a fight ensued between the crews of the two boats, and Kakichi, watching from the breakwater on to which he had just stepped, noted with increasing concern that his uncle was being drawn into the midst of the struggling, fighting men. In an instant Kakichi thrust his body in among them and gripped an oar which was raised to strike his uncle. In his attempt to shield the older man, the oar was brought down with terrific force upon his own head, and in an instant the blue waters of the bay and the faces of the fighting men about him had faded into blackness.

CHAPTER VII

THE DAWN OF LOVE

WHEN THE *Pet Hawk* LOWERED ITS ANCHOR A FEW YARDS
from the white beach of Gamagori, the people of the village were standing at the edge of the surf to welcome its
crew. The sun still shone brightly in a cloudless sky, and
the long shadows of the mast, from which the champion-
ship pennant hung limp, splashed the cobalt-colored surface
of the sea with purple.

"Did you win? Did you win?" shouted Tama, eagerly,
and Yoshie rebuked her, "Don't you see the pennant?" but
her eyes moved quickly, anxiously, over the faces of the
crew. The face she sought was not among them.

"There's been a fight," someone suggested.

"Oh, there's always a fight at these races . . . nothing
serious . . ."

Kakichi's aunt pressed forward. "Sadakichi," she demanded of her husband, anxiously, "where's Kakichi?"

He turned from the prow to answer her. "He's been
hurt. You prepare a bed for him at the house, and get some
hot water ready. We'll bring him right up." His eyes moved
from her face to that of Yoshie, standing close to her side.

"Oh, what happened?" she asked with concern.

"They claimed our boat fouled another. A crowd set on
me and Kakichi stepped between us and received the blow."

"How terrible!"

"He'll be all right in a day or two," Sadakichi comforted

her. "It will probably amount to little more than a head-ache, and after a few days' rest he'll be quite fit again." She was not so easily comforted, however, for it was apparent when six of the crew lifted Kakichi out upon the beach and carried him the short distance to the boat-maker's house that the situation was more grave than Sadakichi had pretended it to be.

"He is as one dead," Yoshie murmured in a low voice, following after the men, her eyes upon Kakichi's bloodless face and bandaged head. She stood silent in the doorway while they laid him on the bed that his aunt had prepared, and spread the quilts over him. One of the men hurried away for a doctor.

Then began for Kakichi a new experience, and one which was to bear definite results, not only in his material, but in his spiritual life. He was, for a week, exceedingly ill, and perhaps because of this fact became something in the nature of a local hero. He developed a high temperature, and the doctor came daily to see him, murmuring vague fears as to blood poisoning. The house was kept very quiet. The young people whom he had met, and many who were interested, knowing his aunt and uncle, came often to inquire about him and to ask whether they might be of any service. Yoshie completely deserted the loom at which she worked to remain continually within reach, running errands, and going for ice to put on his head, and taking from her own purse, which was none too full, enough to buy some rice cakes and fruit and pale, sweet camellia blossoms to place near his bed.

Kakichi wished that he might remain here forever; the trouble and poverty of his own home seemed far away. It would be difficult to return to it. The kindness and love of these people brought quick tears to his eyes, and he turned his face against the pillow to hide them.

In the night he would turn and turn on his bed, hot and feverish, and with the intense pain in his head seeming to increase in the darkness, and it was then that the memory of those few days in the mountains with Kabube-e, and the quiet Sunday evenings that he had spent listening to Mr. Murano, came to his mind. Surely, he thought, now more than ever before, he was a child of God, and no less in His hands because of his suffering. Mr. Murano's God was one of infinite compassion, in whose presence lay the answer to every question even before it was asked, upon whose strength and care one might, at moments like these, trustfully lean. The thought quieted him; he lay very still, listening, holding fast to it. He heard the sound of the waves gently washing the shore, wave after wave in perfect, rhythmic succession. He heard the whispering of the wind in the pines on the hill, and stillness came in upon him. He felt that he was placed entirely in God's care, as were these hills, and the sea in the darkness. On the next day his fever subsided and the pain ceased.

He was more than ever aware, now, of Yoshie's presence in the house. She moved so quietly, and had about her such simplicity and charm, as well as complete naturalness in his presence, that he came to look forward eagerly to those moments when she was near him. When her aunt was not there, she took entire charge of the housework, and from his bed he could watch her as she moved competently about her work. These times when he was alone with her in the house were filled with a singular sweetness. The very fact of her nearness thrilled him, the fact that he might call and she would come at once, her quick concern evident in her sweet face. If he called, and she came, he might reach

out a hand and touch her; yet when she did come, laying
her cool hand gently on his brow, or rubbing his shoulders
easily to remove the ache in them, he could only lie quite
still, feeling in her touch all the beauty of her inmost self
and that loveliness of her soul that manifested itself in her
service.

Yet, he argued with himself, this was surely not a time
in which to fall in love. He had cares and responsibilities;
the time for his military service could not be far off; he
was poor . . . all of these things stood in his path. And
yet, yet he might love her, delighting in her presence, in
the clearness of her eyes and the way his breath caught
when her lashes lay black against her tanned cheek.

Her composure tantalized him; at times it appeared to
him that she was almost unmindful of his presence and he
sought childish pretexts for gaining her attention. When
next she came near him, he vowed, he would most surely
touch her; but he did not.

It was entirely probable that she cared no more for him
than she might for anyone who was ill. She was by nature
loving and kind. It was probable, too, he argued severely,
that when once he went back to the mountains he would
forget her. And yet . . . and yet there was a subtle loveliness about this quiet, gentle girl that suggested that forgetting her might be less simple than he imagined. The fact
that he knew her . . . that she moved and lived in this
same world with him . . . thrilled him.

On the eighth day he made preparations for his departure. He was dizzy, and his head still ached, and the doctor
said that the bandages must remain on his head for two
more weeks, but he was uneasy about his home and about
his work, and felt that he must return to them. He rose
early, and with his aunt's help he packed his few belongings

together. Near the pillow on his bed he was surprised to find
a small envelope. Opening it quickly his eyes went immediately to the signature: "Yoshie!"

"Dear Kakichi, we will be sorry to have you leave us, and
will think of you often when you are back in the mountains. As for me, I shall always love you as a brother. Come
back to us soon." And her name was signed.

"Like a brother." He read and reread the few words.
How he wished he could tell her all that he felt springing
up into life in his heart, putting into words, if he could
only find them, the confusion of his thoughts and yearnings.
But surely he could not speak; the time was not yet. There
was much for him to do first.

"You must eat, Kakichi," his aunt urged, standing at his
side at the breakfast table. "They will say at home that I
have taken poor care of you."

He reached out shyly and took her hand, smiling up at
her. "Oh, they could not say that," he returned, feeling that
these people, who had been almost total strangers little
more than a week ago, were now very close to him, were
indeed a part of his life.

"Well," his aunt observed philosophically, "that is always
the sorrow of making friends; one must part from them at
times."

Tama came to the station, and his uncle and aunt, of
course, and finally Yoshie came when he had given up all
hope of her coming. He leaned out of the train window
and looked down at their upturned faces.

"We shall need you for the races in the spring," Sadakichi
said. "And next time we will see that you are not treated
so badly."

"You could come for the New Year," Tama urged.

"There's always great fun, then." He laughed at their insistence.

"Never fear. I can't say when, but you may be sure I shall come back again," he told them happily, looking over their heads and into the eyes of the girl who stood somewhat in the background.

The whistle blew shrilly; the train began to move slowly. He leaned still farther out of the window to catch one last glimpse of their faces and to hear their friendly good-bys. But it was Yoshie's face upon which he looked last, and took into his memory like a rare and precious thing.

CHAPTER VIII

THE GLOOMY MOUNTAIN HOME

THE ROAD UP THE MOUNTAIN TO TSUGU SEEMED TERRIBLY dark, but, although it was quite late when he arrived home, his mother and Yuriko were both up and welcomed him warmly.

"It's been so lonely without you," Yuriko told him simply, when he had set their fears at rest about his bandaged head and told them of the launching of the new boat and the races.

"We worried about you," his mother added, "and we missed you."

It was good to be missed; it was good to be needed; and more than ever he realized the growth of that need and the responsibility upon him. They had, in his absence, received a letter from the master of Sasuke, Kakichi's brother. His mother's face was anxious and grave as she spoke of it.

"He has been put in prison, Kakichi, and the newspaper has had an account of the arrest. How I have wished that we might hear, now, from your sisters . . . to hear at least that they are well."

While she spoke Kakichi kept his eyes on her face. She must have been a very beautiful girl; with a complexion once as fair as Yuriko's was now, and with no lines of worry and sorrow and poverty drawn upon its fairness. And yet his searching eyes caught on this face a great beauty as she raised her troubled eyes to his. Her love and anxiety for these, her children, shone there like a light within her, more firmly fixed and forever burning than those dim candles that burned on the shelf in the dusk beyond her gray head. What was it Mr. Murano said about Christ being the light of the world . . . the light of men? It was this same light of love that burned in his mother's eyes.

"It may not be as bad as you fear," he sought to comfort her, gently, understanding the disgrace she must feel from having a son in prison. They must find some way of freeing him, for surely he was needed here, at home. Kakichi's thought and hopes sped towards this elder brother; he would undertake the care of this house when he, Kakichi, was called away to service. The command for his examination had in fact arrived.

He read the article in the paper carefully. It was long and had big headlines and told of the rounding up of a gang of delinquent youths. The name of Sasuke was second in the list of sixteen names. The reason for their arrest was given as being the abduction of women, the looting of money and goods, and general disregard for law. Those accused appeared to be operating under the name of a gang known throughout the country for its lawlessness.

Kakichi sighed deeply, although he could not help thinking that half a year ago he himself might easily have come to just such a pass. In his heart he deplored what the city had done to his brother and wished that some simpler life might be accorded them all, by means of which they could wipe out these evils that beset them. There must be some solution. Sasuke must not want to go on in this manner.

"What shall we do?" his mother was saying. "Or is there nothing that we can do? It would seem to me that we must remind him of our thoughts . . ."

"And our prayers . . ." Kakichi added. His face brightened suddenly at a thought.

"Why couldn't we write to my sister Yuki and ask her to go and see him, mother? And that would mean that then we would have word from her, too?"

And so it was agreed that this should be done. Kakichi, in his room, prayed that Sasuke might be brought back to them. God must understand the necessity of this return, since all things were open to Him. In a similar way, all things were opening to Kakichi. Six months ago the sorrows of his family had not mattered to him in the least, nor had any possible way of remedying them suggested itself. Nor would he then have been able to suffer with each of them, and worried about his father and poor misshapen brother, about one imprisoned in illness, and one imprisoned behind walls for lawlessness, and for his sisters whose lives now touched his imagination with deep sorrow. How acute must have been the sufferings and comprehension of the Christ, who had suffered all things with all men!

But the days were filled with activity, with things to be done. He got up each morning early, read his Bible, and when his father was awake, saw that he was washed and shaved and read to him until breakfast. He had managed to put the shop in order, to remove the rubbish from the street, and generally to make the place a great deal neater in appearance. Through all these labors he carried the thought and remembrance of Yoshie with him, yet with the knowledge that this, for the time, was all that he could do.

His mother's concern for Sasuke was only partially relieved when, after more than a week, they received a letter from Kakichi's sister, Yuki.

She wrote that she had made the trip, with difficulties, to the prison in which Sasuke was held. She described her meeting with him and his resignation to the fact that he would have to remain there possibly for several years. As to her own life she said nothing, and if between the lines they sensed a certain hopelessness, this but served to convince them that she should be at home, where her life might assume more of the aspects of normalcy.

Kakichi's heart contracted with pain at his mother's suffering for her children and her wish that she might gather them all together once more. He could find no words to assure her that they would find their rightful place, but he followed her at a distance when she went slowly through the warm rainy night to the small shrine at the base of the village temple to pray.

It had been raining for days, but the air was fresh and clean and filled with the faint fragrance of things growing. All these past days the people of the village had been busy with their rice planting in the flooded fields, so that soon the black earth which had been deserted all through the winter months, and lain fallow, would soon grow green overnight, yielding for those who worked a harvest only large enough to supply them with a meager living. It suddenly occurred to Kakichi how greatly each man's individual life revolved about himself and his own immediate needs and desires. His own had been centered in the disaster of his immediate family. Surely one's service should extend beyond such a limit, reaching out to touch other lives and draw therefrom an added blessing. And yet he was weary, desperately weary, feeling the need for added strength.

He looked up at the hills dimly outlined against the sky in the early darkness. Some of their power and strength seemed to flow down to him as he sat there; some of their resolute quietude was his own. He caught his breath, suddenly, with the wonder of the answer to his need. However much his life might manifest disaster, something seemed to say to him that with each new experience there would be new life and power born into him. A life enriched by the very suffering that would seem to destroy it, the very poverty that suggested its end . . . this was a life built on an enduring rock. Ships might be tossed and wrecked on the face of the waters, in the midst of the storm, but underneath in the depths there was stillness. Underneath there was peace. This stillness and peace must be lifted up into being, into an ever-present reality.

Within a few days this half-formed wish to be of even greater service had its reward.

Kakichi was obliged to go almost daily to the Kurino dispensary to have his bandage changed. He had first attempted to do this for himself, but the wound had not changed as quickly as he had expected. The doctor's waiting room was always crowded with patients, and it was difficult for Kakichi to wait his turn. He therefore asked if it might not be possible for him to come early in the evening, and to this the doctor had kindly agreed. These visits began to be increasingly important in Kakichi's life. His contacts with men of the doctor's type were necessarily limited, and in the brief conversations that ensued during these visits his horizon was extended, his interest in local and national affairs stimulated, and his own self-confidence and ability to speak more freely greatly increased. The doctor began to take a real and friendly interest in this young man, of whom Mr. Murano spoke with such esteem. He had, even in the short time since he had known him, shown such a marked improvement that he could not forbear speaking of it.

"This village needs young men like you, Kakichi," he told him. "There is a great deal to be done, and so pitifully few who will do it. I know that the trials of your own household seem oppressing, but those things are for a reason. How you bear them will react upon the community, and the respect and commendation of one's neighbors is, I think, something to be highly valued. So that all that you are doing is not unmarked, nor will it be unrewarded. I feel certain of that, and so does Mr. Murano. Even in the short time that you have been home there has been a change, not only in your ideals, but in your very face and speech and manner."

Kakichi felt his face flush warmly at such sincere praise.

"Besides," continued the good doctor kindly, "your family's stress of circumstances is light in comparison with that of others."

"It is just that they seem so heavy at times," Kakichi reflected.

"I know." He paused. "Perhaps in doing things for those in greater need . . ." he began thoughtfully. "By the way, do you know the lodginghouse in the upper part of the village? The one called the Yamano House?"

"Yes. I know that place."

"Well," continued the doctor, "behind that house there is a family of lepers living in a shed."

"Lepers?" exclaimed Kakichi incredulously.

"Yes. Four years ago the father came here to work on one of the roads as a laborer, and he had been here only a short while when he was taken ill. At first he lay in the Yamano House, but when it was discovered what his illness was, he was put out. There was no place to go, so he went into the miserable little shed to live. He sent back to his home village for his wife, and there they have been living, with their two children. She died two weeks ago, and those children are hardly able to look after their father. The village authorities will do nothing about it. Murano and I have been trying to place the children in an orphanage and the father in some asylum, but nothing has been accomplished. No one will go near him to help him."

"It would seem," Kakichi said, "as though something should be done."

"Murano and I saw that the wife was buried; the boys are only eight and five. How they will manage I cannot see. We cannot even arrange for their schooling. Between the two of us we have managed to look after them, although with my practice I fear that the bulk of responsibility has fallen on Murano."

Kakichi did not go directly home that night. He walked along the outskirts of the village and on in the direction of the shed behind the Yamano House. It had been a shed used for the storage of charcoal and was like a cave, with no window, and only a very narrow door. A child, who was eating something out of a box, sat crouched in the doorway. A dim lantern burned inside. Kakichi stopped. His own house surely seemed a fortunate place in which to live in comparison with this poor place.

"Could I see your father?" he asked suddenly. An older, and obviously undernourished, boy came out of the shed. The boys stared at him with round, wondering dark eyes. He repeated his question:

"But he cannot move; he is in bed," the older one replied at last.

"Yes, I know. The doctor told me about him." But still he hesitated. If Mr. Murano and the doctor entered in at this door, then surely he might enter.

His eyes were not at first accustomed to the semidarkness, but he noted a torn straw matting on the earthen floor, and the dim, distorted face of a man on a low bed in the corner. A straw peaked hat, such as beggars use on the street, hung from a peg on the wall. Kakichi stood back, uncertain, his horrified eyes moving away from the man's sick eyes to the rudely constructed god-shelf above the bed.

"I came to see how you were," he began; and then continued, still uncomfortably, "I'm one of the village folk and thought that I might do something for you." But what he could do, he surely did not know. The man could not talk. Kakichi's impulse was to run from the room, and it was only by making a tremendous effort that he remained where he was. He turned to look at the children who had followed him in and were watching him curiously, their eyes tremendous in their starved little faces. Kakichi's eyes filled with tears; these children must be fed. The weight of their plight lay heavy upon him, as did his helplessness. The Bible said that Jesus had placed his hands upon a leper; *he* could not do that. He would never be able to do that. He hastily drew from his pocket two small coins and laid them on a small wooden box crudely constructed near the bed. He knew of nothing else to do. Turning to the doorway he came face to face with Mr. Murano.

"Hullo there!" the older man greeted him with obvious surprise, his face suddenly tender. "I hadn't expected to find you here, Kakichi, and yet when I think of it I know of no one better fitted than you to come here."

"Better fitted?" Kakichi said unbelievingly. "What can I do here?"

"Oh, a great deal. Wait, and walk back to the village with me, won't you?" And Kakichi waited, standing back curiously intent to watch what he would do. He went first to the sick man, talking to him all the while, and remaking the bed with as much skill as any woman might have. Then he opened a package which he had brought with him and prepared to give him a hypodermic injection. With perfect ease and gentleness he cleansed the man's arm. Kakichi came nearer, still watching, his discomfiture vanishing.

"This is an oil, good for leprosy, and must be injected every day. Kurino taught me, so that I could relieve him."

"And what," proceeded Kakichi helplessly, "is there for me to do?"

"For the moment," Mr. Murano suggested, "you could sweep out the shed. There is a need for a window in here; do you suppose, some day, you could do that?"

Kakichi nodded eagerly, watching him as he carefully disinfected his hands. He was filled with admiration for the man's skill. As he walked back through the village with him he felt, more than ever, his desire to imitate him. Here, surely, were works, not just words. Well, he at least might go and sweep.

"Will that man live for some time?" he asked, feeling that such a life could surely not long be possible.

"He may. He has an astonishing will to live."

"That seems almost beyond belief," Kakichi murmured. "It would seem to me that death would be far more welcome than such an existence."

"Life is no less precious to a man because he is retarded in the race. It is never less than a spark sent from God, and it may still hold a victory to his imagination. All sorts of things happen that God's glory may be demonstrated, if not in our own lives, then in those with whom we come in contact. We would all be much further along if we recognized this as divine guidance and were more submissive to it, seeing in the pattern a means of effecting a triumphant end."

A triumphant end! How grandly those words rang

through his memory in the next days! How ardent was his desire for such a clear vision for himself and for others!

Now, each time he went to the doctor's he went also to the leper's shed. Each time he had less fear; each time he saw more things for him to do. Each time a greater blessing seemed to follow his service, until, after a few weeks, he was taking his turn at giving the injections, despite his mother's violent opposition. He attempted to tell her that he felt a secure and divine protection. Her complaints finally evaporated, and soon she was managing to put away a small portion of food each week for the leper and his children, and contriving to lay aside a few pennies for Kakichi to take them.

And now it was the rainy season. The whole village seemed wrapped in a thin mist of rain. The road to the mountain village was thick with mud so that the carts did not travel on it, and for days at a time no traveler walked that way. When, one gray day, as the clouds hung low and heavy over the hills, a woman walked up the street, the men in the forge left their work to stare through the steaming window.

She was beautiful; the men at the forge admired her painted cheeks and reddened mouth, although Kakichi, staring curiously with the others, failed to find in these things his answer to beauty. She was, very plainly, a stranger in the village. But there was about her something that made one of them call out to her in an overfriendly tone, at which she turned her head and smiled. Kakichi stood very still, looking at her over the shoulders of his fellows.

"Who is that?" Totaro asked curiously, the long fire

tongs in his hands. The men shook their heads. She walked to the door of the house next the forge.

"I think," said Kakichi quietly, "that that must be my sister, come home. How happy my mother will be!" The men stared at him over the red-hot sheet of iron upon which he was hammering, but made no answer.

CHAPTER IX

PAINT AND POWDER'S INERTIA

KAKICHI'S MOTHER'S JOY IN YUKI'S RETURN WAS SHORT-LIVED. She was quite openly disgusted with the plight of the household, and held for her father and Taiji more of a disgusted forbearance than of pity. Her knowledge did not include any understanding of the sick or the maimed, nor, for that matter, of the wretchedness of humanity.

She had been sold originally because she possessed a personal beauty which was rare for a mountain girl. By reason of it she had held for ten years the doubtful position she now occupied. It had consumed all of her time and all of her interests, so that she was, Kakichi decided after a short time, no more than a face and a body.

She stayed in bed late in the mornings, and her hours when she was awake were spent in putting compresses upon her face, then thick layers of powder and sticky red paint on her lips. She fretted continually because the village hairdresser proved unequal to her demands. She was middle-aged and frightened, and, to Kakichi's increasingly observant mind, infinitely pathetic. He could see no beauty in her painted face, nor seduction in her slovenly attired person. She was utterly useless to his mother, and extremely bewildering.

Her language was rough and uncouth, her complaints as to the surroundings and the food unceasing, and she did nothing to remedy either. Her mother looked at her with hurt and wondering eyes. Kakichi only by effort remained silent, until he discovered that she had sent Yuriko out upon two occasions at night to buy rice wine, on the pretext that she was going to give it to her father.

She turned on him in a fury that distorted and aged her face. "What is it to you?" she demanded. "They tell me in the village that you have become a Christian. Does my mother know that? If any punishment has come to this house, it is because you have disgraced our ancestors with your beliefs."

Her mother stared helplessly from one to the other. An attempt to argue with her would surely prove more than futile, Kakichi decided, but he observed quietly that the Christian religion, even as little as he had imbibed thus far, taught one love and reverence for one's parents that seemed, to him, at least, more effective than a worship of the dead.

"You can believe what you please," Yuki answered, "but there is no reason to tell me what to do. In this Christian religion one can neither smoke nor drink." She laughed loudly. "If everyone put this into practice how dull it would be! And if they never went to the licensed quarters, how would I live?"

"I'm sure I don't know," Kakichi said, "unless you discovered that there *was* another way."

How she had managed to leave and when she would return were details she did not discuss with them. The fact that she had brought no luggage was reason to believe that her stay would be limited. But what, to Kakichi's mind, was more to the point was that her presence brought nothing in the nature of a blessing to the house, nor did they in any way seem to influence her. She was bitterly defensive when a telegram came from her master, demanding her whereabouts. She tore it to bits, laughing at Kakichi's concern.

"Don't worry," she counseled, "they won't send the police for me. There's no reason why I should go back; I've paid off all my debts to him."

"Then why didn't you bring your things and gain his permission to leave?"

She evaded his questions.

"And," pursued Kakichi with deliberation, "if your debts are placed on our shoulders we will not be able to meet them."

She looked at him and turned grave for a moment. "I suppose you'll find a way. As for me, I don't really care what becomes of me."

This was his opportunity; he leaned forward eagerly. "Oh, but *we* do, Yuki. There are so many things you might do," he said kindly.

Her fingers, brown with cigarette stains, arranged the thick coils of her hair as she listened.

"There's always a place for one if you mean to go forward."

"Even if you think you're going to do right, the world is so evil you don't gain anything by keeping straight," was her observance.

"You surely have enough courage to live decently; you have lived long enough in the other manner and it has brought you nothing." But she would not listen. However, when a second telegram from her master announced that he was getting a court writ for her return, he felt that she must make some decision as to what would be done. For Masa was worried. If they were to be involved financially because of Yuki's debts, or even if the authorities would come to the house to get her . . . these things happening in so small a community would hardly be creditable to them. And it had seemed, lately, that things were more hopeful.

But Yuki could give them no satisfaction as to what had transpired. That it was a legal offense to leave one's master she admitted, but she would not discuss it. "If I am going to be taken to task in this way, I'll leave the house," she told them furiously. "I have come home in my attempt to be respectable, but if I am to be given no peace here, I'll go." She tossed a half-smoked cigarette out the door.

There were tears on her mother's cheeks and her voice was broken. "But we wanted you at home, Yuki. It was our wish."

"I can make a home of my own," she flung at them disdainfully. "I have a lover." Masa raised troubled eyes.

"A lover?" Kakichi repeated.

"Of course. How stupid you are, Kakichi! You were always slow and dull."

He paid no attention to that. "You mean that he wants to marry you?" This, after all, would assure her a home and care. He simply could not face the thought of going away within a few months and leaving this problem with his mother for solution. Oh, if only . . . if only Sasuke were at home, and as the elder son took his place at the head of this household in his, Kakichi's, enforced absence!

"What does your lover do?" his mother inquired hesitantly.

"He's a newspaper reporter; it was he who urged me to come home."

"And you are promised to marry each other?" Kakichi continued. She nodded. But somehow he did not believe her, and neither, he thought, did his mother.

So quickly did the answer follow the question that it was

less than a week, one hot, muggy afternoon, that Sasuke
came home.

Kakichi was at work, and this time there was no one to
note a stranger's arrival. He entered the shop, a tall young
man with long black hair, a grim stern face, a thin hard
mouth. He wore a gray blouse such as Russian communists
wear, ragged trousers and badly torn shoes. Immediately
upon entering the shop, which was empty, he dropped down
wearily upon the floor behind the counter, and fell into a
deep sleep of exhaustion.

Masa found him there. He lay in the shadow of the
counter and she did not at once recognize him as her son.
She stood for a moment in the doorway, frightened, staring
at him in perplexity.

"Who is that?" she demanded, and he awoke, sat up and
looked at her.

"Why, it's Sasuke," she exclaimed, and came toward him
quickly, her face shining. "But why do you lie here, my
son? Why didn't you tell me that you had come back? I
hardly knew you, as you lay sleeping there."

He stood up, grunting something unintelligible.

"Then there was some mistake about your being in prison
for a year. Well, that is reason for rejoicing," she continued.
"We have needed you here, Sasuke."

"I got out on bail," he told her. "I had no money for
fare, so I walked."

"Walked! But it is fifty miles, Sasuke!" She leaned forward anxiously. "You must be weary. I will heat water for
you and get food. And you must take off your shoes." She
bent over to draw off his torn shoes, but his hand brushed
her aside impatiently.

"Kakichi and I have been anxious about you," she continued, in an effort to conceal the small hurt his unconcern

caused her. "We wanted to come to see you, but there seemed to be no way. Your father has been ill, and Taiji too. So Kakichi asked Yuki to come to visit you."

He pushed back the long hair out of his eyes.

"Yuki? A newspaper reporter came, saying he had been sent by her."

His mother realized instantly that Yuki had lied, but she made no attempt to pursue the matter at this time. Just then Yuki appeared, having just come in from the barber-shop across the street.

"Well! This is Sasuke, isn't it? What's the matter with you?"

"Matter? Why?" he snapped.

"He has walked a long distance and is tired," her mother interrupted. "Come, Sasuke, and lie down in the back room. A customer may come in." Yuki laughed. But he followed his mother into the back room. When he had washed and eaten, he fell asleep again. Masa stared at him as he lay, breathing heavily, on some piles of matting in the corner. His body was thick and heavy; there was some-thing lifeless about him that frightened her. He looked so strange, so different . . . this, her son. She could have wept for him.

She was even more distressed, however, later that after-noon when there was another addition to her household. Without any explanation, Yuki introduced a young man, similar in appearance to Sasuke and with the long hair and peculiar blouse he effected, as Sugita, who had very obvi-ously, and with the greatest composure, come to stay. It was at once apparent that he was the "lover" of whom Yuki had spoken, and that he and Yuki and Sasuke were going to be mutually congenial.

And so it happened that when Kakichi returned that

evening, after he had made his usual visit to the leper, he was somewhat startled to find the household considerably increased. His joy in having Sasuke home was immediately eclipsed by Sasuke's insufferable manner. He was the head of the house now, and as such meant to show his authority. But further than this he did not go; he made no attempt to contribute to the depleted resources of the family. Neither he nor Sugita made any effort to secure any work. They loafed all through the day and drank great quantities of rice wine, and when their money for this was exhausted, they charged it. This infuriated Kakichi; he could find neither excuse nor explanation for their actions. He had built high hopes on this elder brother's return, and the futility of human planning was more than ever apparent. In later days he came to recognize, however, that out of these troubled weeks had come a blessing that was to affect all his later life, as well as that of the village.

For it was on a June evening, two weeks after Sasuke's arrival, that Kakichi decided that there was no longer a place for him in his home.

He had returned from the service at Mr. Murano's, to which he had gone with a heavy heart, to find the three of them drinking wine in the kitchen. Generally they let him alone, but to-night Sasuke was ugly. He made an attempt to stop Kakichi as he passed through the room on his way upstairs.

"Come and join us, Kakichi. Have some wine!" urged Sasuke, unsteadily proffering a tall cup.

"I'm sorry, but I don't drink wine." He would have gone on up the stairs, but Sasuke's heavy hand pulled him back. Yuki and Sugita sat back enjoying the scene.

"And why not? You'd be better for some wine in your blood," scoffed Sasuke. "You've forgotten your manners in my absence. When your older brother offers you a drink, it is not customary to refuse it. Drink!" And he pressed the cup against the younger man's mouth.

Kakichi's face was white, his hands clenched at his side. And this was the brother in whom he had placed such faith!

"You're an insolent fellow," Sasuke maintained, his face purple with rage at the boy's composure. Yuki and Sugita laughed shrilly. "When I was in prison you never once wrote. Since I have been home you have done nothing to welcome me. You seem to forget that I am heir to this house."

There flashed into Kakichi's mind the thought: Your inheritance is not of this world; and he knew that what was his, spiritually, was intact and safe, and no man could take it from him. He stood straighter with the thought; the color came back into his face and the hands at his sides relaxed.

But Sasuke continued, still holding him fast: "I hear that you think yourself a Christian, and I tell you, as eldest son of this house, that you might as well lay aside this foolishness. It is an ignorant superstition, and we will be the laughingstock of the village. This belief in one called Christ is no more than a deception of the bourgeois class." He sounded as though, despite his drunkenness, he was quoting, and Kakichi stared at him.

But his mother had come down the stairs, hearing the loud voice of her son, and she came now, quietly, to stand between them, and to lay her roughened hand on Sasuke's restraining one.

"And if you shout so, Sasuke," she said with a gentleness that surprised Kakichi, "it is you who will make us ridiculous in the eyes of our neighbors. You have a right to come to your house, it is yours, but you have no right to abuse Kakichi. He has not the slightest intention of taking anything that is yours. As if there was anything to take, with sickness in the house, and debts to be paid! Without Kakichi we would have nothing to eat to-morrow. You speak as you do because you are drunk."

He turned on her. "I am not drunk. I speak this way because his manner needs correcting. He has shown me no deference since I've been at home."

"It is he who has wanted you back more than any of us," his mother told him, "because he hoped the most."

"And I suppose he hopes to inherit the store," Yuki interrupted angrily. "How about the stock there, and the credit which the store has built up?"

"Neither of you speaks with any understanding," Masa said suddenly, wearily, and turned away. Kakichi watched her, never having loved her as he did at that moment. There was for the moment, he felt, no place for him here. So he went, that same night, to Mr. Murano's house, and they took him in and kept him.

CHAPTER X

THE LANES THROUGH THE MULBERRY FIELDS

FOR A LONG WHILE IT WAS NOT APPARENT TO KAKICHI WHAT blessing could lay in the return of his brother and sister to their home. But had they never come back, and by their conduct so displaced him temporarily, he would never have known the happy hours he was to spend at Mr. Murano's, the tremendous significance of his relationship with this godlike man, and the results that were to ensue. For here, now for the first time, he came to voice his own growing beliefs, and in the sharing of them was to find his own convictions grow apace.

The people who came to this house were serious, steady people. Sometimes he was content to listen; sometimes, and with greater ease and frequency, he could speak. But it was to Mr. Murano that he first related Kakube-e's dream for the development of the mountain land. In his effort to offset his family's impoverished condition, he had come to see in this a salvation not alone for himself and his neighbors, but for Japan. His imagination had been kindled at the thought of work supplied to all men, and food, and a common cause. The starved land cried out for care with a need no less important than the individual's, and synonymous with the individual's.

"And yet," he added wistfully, "how can these things be accomplished? Kakube-e is a hermit and has nothing but this dream of his. And I . . . I have not even an education."

"You have faith; you have learned to pray. This is enough. All the rest will follow. We need not know how or why or when. It is a good dream, and it is for the good of all; therefore, it is bound to come true."

And so Kakichi held fast to it.

It became clear to him in these days that, whatever might have been his hopes regarding Sasuke, the latter was far from ready to assume the responsibility of this household of his. It was evident, too, that Yuki had come home for no other reason than that she had had no other place to go. Unlike the prodigal son, they felt no need to be taken into the love that home typified; they had come back filled with their own ideas. If the ground here proved barren, they would go elsewhere, since their need for rightful things did not exist.

Yuki and Sugita left first, after an officer came with orders for Yuki to report immediately at the Taguchi police station, an order at which she, as well as Sugita and Sasuke, laughed contemptuously. And that same night Yuki and Sugita disappeared.

Sasuke roamed the countryside. Sometimes he was loquacious as to what possible errand he might be on, but more often he was sullen and drunken and only abusive. He had, he said, a mission; he had a message to deliver to both landowners and tenant farmers, but what the content of such a message might be Kakichi could not rightly discover. Sasuke spoke of an "age of imposture and deceit" and the "right to resist law and order." On the day when Kakichi went to take his physical examination for conscription, and was informed that he was in the first class and would be due for conscription early in the coming year,

Sasuke was bitter in his denunciations of any law that could command obedience in this fashion.

"It would be better if you would go down to the mill and find work," his mother told him as she listened doubtfully to his angry protests.

"Work! The more you work, the more the capitalist class is able to extort from you. My interest must be sacrificed for the sake of class propaganda," was his reply, and one for which she knew no answer. These were new phrases, and unfamiliar to her ears. "See how little Kakichi gains for all his work, and his contribution to society is nothing. When he goes to war, it will be even less," he mocked.

"Obedience is a duty," she found words to say, and went to see Mata, the miller, to ask if there might be work picking mulberry leaves for him. But Sasuke would not hear of this. He continued to go about the countryside by day, and he would send Yuriko to the wineshop every night. How this bill would be paid, Kakichi did not know, but that he himself would have to pay it he was certain. He came home more and more reluctantly, realizing the futility of argument, and unwilling to listen long to Sasuke's insolent jeers and drunken revolutionary speeches. If he came home late, it meant that he could do no more than sleep; his reading to his father had to be discontinued. The house was too upset, too much a place of worriment for any quiet to enter in. It was easier not to return at all; Mr. Murano's was a veritable refuge.

One Sunday evening late in June a man who had come to lecture on the Bible, and who was visiting the Muranos, taught Kakichi a lesson that was to be remembered well in the coming months. Kakichi spoke of his desire for education and of the obstacles presented by his circumstances and his urgent necessity to make a living. This man told him

how, as a boy, he had held a position as office boy in a
school, and how every evening he had gone to a night
school of electrical engineering, taking examinations year
after year until his scholastic attainments were on a par
with those of a graduate of the Imperial University. "There
are books here," the man added, indicating Mr. Murano's
extensive library, "that would contribute more to this education you yearn for than weeks in a school. Take them,
then, and read," he urged, and Mr. Murano seconded this
idea.

Towards the very end of the month Sasuke received a
summons from the District Court. The reason for it was
not made clear, but that it was urgent there could be little
doubt. He would need money for this trip, he said, and
appealed to his mother and to Kakichi. There was not
enough money in the house, however, for his need.

"I have only two days left in which to appear," Sasuke
argued petulantly. "I need only ten yen. It would seem that
you could get that small sum for me."

But ten yen was no small sum for one who was earning
only one a day. And the knowledge of the wine Sasuke
consumed every evening, and of the bill to be paid for it,
rankled in Kakichi's breast. If his brother had put by what
he had wasted in wine, the money to go to Nagoya would
have been a mere trifle. Kakichi was silent.

So Sasuke stealthily carried the bedquilts under which
he had been sleeping to the pawnshop in the village. He
received less, however, than the amount necessary to take
him to Nagoya. Very early on the morning of the next day
he approached his mother once again.

"Surely you must have some money in your purse," he
said coaxingly. "And it may be that I shall not be coming
back again."

Slowly she opened her purse. On the preceding night Kakichi had given her some money which he had borrowed for Sasuke from Mr. Murano. It was more than would be needed for the journey, alone. She handed him a bill, gravely, her voice hushed by all her fears for him gathered like a knot in her breast.

"You should not have taken our quilts," she remonstrated gently. "We need them."

"But I told you I needed money. Surely you have more than this," he complained. She turned for a moment to look out through the window at the sky growing light in the east, and then turning back, without a word emptied her purse into his outstretched hand.

"Take it all, then!" she told him, when without thanks he would have gone. "You will be troubled, however far you may travel, and no amount of wine you will drink will drown your sorrow. Of that I am certain, Sasuke."

And he went out immediately, and without farewell, to wait for the early morning bus to Nagoya.

The house seemed quiet when he had gone. For the first time Kakichi noticed a definite change in his father, who despite his inability to speak, still managed to convey to them his happiness at this return to the old routine. His condition was no better, but he was patient and uncomplaining; the wine bottle at his side was untouched. Over these things Kakichi silently rejoiced and gave thanks.

His mother and Yuriko were busy, these days, feeding silkworms for market. They had undertaken this work, hoping thereby to add to the resources of the family. In the early morning hours Kakichi would go with them to the fields to pick mulberry leaves. It was his prayer and desire to restock the shop once again with the money thus earned, trusting that in the days of his absence it might bring in a better return. But the fields where they gathered leaves promised, as usual, an insufficient supply, and both his mother and sister were utterly disheartened.

Early one morning, with this need paramount in his mind, Kakichi laid his big basket down in the lane in the field as he paused for a moment in prayer. His need was for leaves, and yet how he wished, too, that he might see in all these happenings of the past months and weeks some plan unfolding for good, some promise of recompense for those who were dear to him! If only his vision might be clear enough to discern a pattern in the tangled strands! For Mr. Murano assured him that the promises of the Bible were no less sure in his life, because for the moment they seemed invisible. He would be led by paths that he knew not; all that was crooked would be made straight. A deeper quietude possessed him.

Just then Mata, the owner of the mill, turned the corner of the narrow lane. Kakichi raised his head. The man stopped.

"Oh, good morning," Mata said cordially. "Nice day, isn't it?" and he looked up at the clear morning sky. He had on the peculiar disreputable-looking hunting cap he invariably wore, and his beard was disheveled as usual, and yet Kakichi knew that he was, despite his appearance, highly respected in the community, not only as a big land-owner and president of the Silk Growers' Association, but as a man of intelligence and exceptional business ability. His manner was sometimes gruff and outspoken, but he was reputed among his tenants to be always just and kindly. It was from him that Kakichi's mother rented the mulberry fields in which they picked.

"Yes, it is a fine day," Kakichi agreed pleasantly.

"You are attaining a certain respect in the village,

Kakichi," the miller continued unexpectedly. "I am glad to hear good things of you; your elder brother gave me a lot of trouble. He stirred things up considerably in a tenancy dispute over at Taguchi, and the owners of the farm there, who are relatives of mine, have not been able to collect the rice to be paid over as land rent for last year. They were just reaching a compromise on the deduction of three-tenths of the crop when your brother came along and upset the plans by telling them they did not need to pay a single cent of rent, and inciting them not to do so. But I hear that he has gone, now?"

"Yes, he has gone. And it is unfortunate that he came to do that," Kakichi said sincerely.

"Well, I respect a man's opinions when his actions seem to justify that respect," was Mata's terse comment. He paused and then continued, "It looks to me as though you wouldn't have quite enough leaves," he said, scanning the field critically. "Why not come into our field and have some of ours, for we will have more than we need?"

A great wave of gladness and joy swept over Kakichi as he listened, and his heart was lifted to the very sky's deep, pure blue. How quick this answer to his prayer had come! Quicker than light itself!

Words tumbled out hastily in his attempt to express his gratitude.

"Come along and get some any time," Mata repeated genially. "I don't want any pay for the leaves." And he nodded and moved off down the lane, taking from his pocket an ancient and worn tobacco pouch and preparing to smoke.

In Bible times, Kakichi thought, looking after him, according to the Old Testament, the Lord God caused water to spring forth and saved the life of Elijah the prophet when he was athirst and prayed under the juniper tree. And he, too, must have shared this same joyousness that Kakichi felt, warm and vital and flowing through his whole being. As he listened, the mockingbirds sang with renewed wildness in the green groves, so that all the morning was abrim with birdsong and light. Here, in this corner of the field, was surely heaven, and a heaven that he might carry with him into the dark forge of the blacksmith's shop.

He paused for a moment more, tasting on his lips the sweetness of the morning, and of his oneness with a great beneficent Purpose. How much these short months had accomplished for him; not only a change in his manner and appearance, for he was aware, with others, of these things, minor though they might be. He knew that he lifted his head when he spoke, and that, more steadily, he was lifting his thoughts with his words. The enjoyments of a year ago were unimportant now, and life was, despite its manifold restrictions, infinitely richer and more abundantly satisfying. He could not but rejoice that day by day through the good hand of God, often unrealized, his soul as well as all his dreams and desires were being lifted into the purer atmosphere of spirit. He was conscious that within his own breast there was being built up the foundation of a high moral purpose, not alone for himself and those dependent upon him, but for those in the same village, in the same land.

From the hilltop where he stood he could see the mulberry fields, deserted and barren of all save their stalks, and far to the south, on the side of the mountain, the land was brown and bare and empty of life. And yet these were the places in which Kakube-e sought transformation, from which he thought growth might spring! This barren, depleted wilderness! There was to Kakichi's eyes, as he looked, a sudden illusion of light on these waste places, counterpart of that light within himself. The sun poured through a break in the clouds, an effulgent water from a great vessel. Almost like a blessing, he thought, catching his breath sharply as he looked. Reluctantly he turned his eyes away, as from something too bright, and looked down upon the roofs of the village houses. It was hard to realize that this, his own mountain village, with the beauty of the hills lifted as a constant challenge and stimulus at its door, should be so dissolute, so lost in poverty and immorality.

Cafés had recently been opened where the young people might gather, and they came up from the lower village for the purpose. Their reputation was unsavory; they were rendezvous for the restless. They bred, night after night, new excitements, all purposeless at best.

His own home bore such dire evidence of the effect of just such an influence that Kakichi thought desperately of some way in which a similar catastrophe might be averted from any other life in this lovely village. As he thought of the manner of life in the various homes, he was deeply convinced that the farming villages were through just such influences falling into deeper poverty and misery. Surely, his thoughts continued, through the lives of individuals, rightly guided by Christian principles, these towns might be lifted into a happier realization of being. Christ had so liberally promised the Kingdom of God to those who believed. Well, *he* believed, did he not? What, then, was the service that he might render, outside of his own duty as a son and a brother? Well, he might begin with the one thing that had come to his mind, the thing which he felt was most responsible for his own home's misfortune. He might start a Temperance Society with certain young men of the village, men from Mr. Murano's class. They would be with him. The way might not seem clear in which this was to be accomplished, but if his purpose was sure the way would be opened to his sight. The morning's experience had convinced him of that.

And as he came down the mountain he was conscious with every step that he had been given a new and sustaining strength.

CHAPTER XI

A Silver-colored Lantern

THERE WAS NOW ANOTHER, AND MORE PERSONAL PROBLEM OF strength and sense of inner victory, for, as he passed by the doorway of his own home to enter that of the forge, he encountered a policeman who had obviously been waiting for him. He saw Jinnosuke lean out from the window of the blacksmith's shop, to stare curiously. Kakichi stopped.

"You are the brother of Sasuke, are you not?"

What could have happened now? Kakichi thought. He nodded. "Yes, I am his brother. Is he in trouble?"

"He is a bad lot, this brother of yours," the policeman continued, his black eyes fixed on Kakichi's face.

Kakichi waited.

"He's accused of burglary and of killing a policeman in Nagoya," the man continued steadily. Kakichi winced, and, turning his head on a sudden impulse, his eyes met those of his mother, standing in the doorway, her basket of leaves upon her arm. He knew from the sight of her white face that she had heard, and instinctively he moved nearer to her, as though to ward off this blow that fell hardest of all upon her.

"It is of no great merit to you to have a criminal in your family," the policeman was continuing unsympathetically. "And a bad mark, too, on our local records."

"We would have stopped him if we could have," Kakichi

answered, feeling an overwhelming pity for Sasuke, his much-vaunted freedom now quite dissolved.

The man grunted. "You can tell me something of his habits while he was here," he ordered.

"He left because of a summons . . ."

"He didn't appear in court. He was evidently in need of money, although it is known that he spent some in a wine-shop, and he held up a young man in the early evening on a little-known thoroughfare of Nagoya. When he was caught by a policeman, he stabbed him in the scuffle that followed. He was carrying a knife."

Kakichi said, "Yes?" There was no sound from his mother, only her quickened breathing, as if she were in pain.

"That's all. He's where he won't be bothering people for quite a while. But his habits . . . he drank a lot? And stole I suppose?"

They made no answer.

"Radical, too, isn't he?"

And his mother answered this time, brokenly: "Even as a child he liked to pretend he was a hero, and he was always rushing around saying that he was helping the weak. He is like that still," she forgave him.

The tears came hotly to Kakichi's eyes as he listened. How bitter must be the knowledge in her heart that her son was a murderer, how keen her shame in this small village where her years had been such a struggle, and where things like this counted heavily against one.

At the forge it was discussed, and the report which came out in the paper satisfied the curious. But Kakichi went about his work without comment, not unaware, however, of all they said.

"Sasuke was always a bad lot, and so was his father before him."

"Yes. It's surely no more than can be expected in a home of that kind."

How he wanted to say to them that they should come and see what manner of home it now was . . . poor enough, perhaps, but with calm and orderliness emerging out of chaos, a dim hope glimpsed where there had been only despair. No one could be reborn, and not carry the marks of it into his home. But the time was not yet when they would come, or see. They saw only the outer side of the picture . . . not the thought that lay beneath and that would emerge more surely when the vision was clear enough. And, he admitted, the outside of the picture was more than the mind could contemplate for very long. He had to shift his gaze quickly, to a Reality, that through persistent faith he would bring down into being.

He caught a glimpse of his mother climbing the steps and coming up into the yard. She had a pole across her shoulders, which bent with the weight of the branches hung from each end. If one looked at these evidences of faith and strength and forbearance as God must look at them, how white must be the light of such a victory! How sure and rich the reward!

Christ had endured! And his travail had not completed the work of redemption begun nineteen hundred years ago. It cried out, still, for more souls to share the vision. All these things, indeterminate bits of a seemingly dark pattern, were parts of a whole, forming for some future time and race the nucleus of a more perfect picture, a more perfect world. Each man's groping carried him, and his brother, nearer the Kingdom of Heaven. But one's vision must cease to be mortal, and become Infinite. Then only did all assume the aspects of beauty, as the dim lines of a picture when one stands back to look upon it.

In the days that followed Kakichi held steadily to these thoughts, putting into his service to his father and the leper a renewed spirit of love and humility. Whenever he entered the dark shed where the sick man lay, he had invariably had a sense of fear, but this was gone now. He found time to make a new window, and to place the sick man so that he could look out.

He found time, too, to broach to Mr. Murano, who since Sasuke's trouble had appeared in the papers showed an even greater interest in Kakichi and his affairs, his thoughts about a Temperance Society. The young minister was immediately enthusiastic.

"How I have been wishing for just such a thing in this village; there is such a need for it, but we have always lacked someone to take the lead. Why haven't I thought of it?"

Just one week later they heard that Yamada Yoshinobu, the famous pioneer and champion of the Village Temperance Movement, was coming to lecture in a nearby town. This seemed to be, then, the time to begin. Accordingly a telegram was dispatched and a satisfactory answer received, and a crusade begun for village prohibition.

After countless difficulties a place was secured in which to hold the meeting, and large posters printed and hung about the village. They caught the attention of the passers-by successfully for just one day. By the next day there was not one left; they had been ripped from the posts on which they were hung. Jinnosuke, who was always well acquainted with all village happenings, reported that the miscreant had been the owner of the town's leading café.

On the next day, however, Kakichi went around once again pasting up more posters of the same sort.

There were only twenty people at that first meeting, and they had come, it was true, more out of curiosity than real interest. But they had come! Yamada's lecture was a detailed report of the actual results in those villages in Japan which had adopted prohibition, and the particular benefits derived in the villages given over to agricultural pursuits. What he said could not fail to make a deep impression upon those who, like Kakichi, were vitally interested, but how widely shared this initial interest might be it was difficult, at once, to see. However, the meeting had a direct result, for a Temperance Society was brought into being in the village, and Kakichi was elected as head of it. He protested, feeling that he was not the one to whom this honor should be given, feeling, too, that his own family's misdeeds were against him, in light of public favor, but Mr. Murano overruled his refusal.

"This movement will never succeed unless there is someone very earnest and sincere and humble behind it," Mr. Murano insisted, "and I know of no one better fitted than you, Kakichi."

The Kurino Dispensary was to be their official headquarters, and Mr. Murano and Kakichi took the main part of the work of the office.

According to custom in the villages, signs were hung from the houses whose occupants avowed temperance, and on that first evening when a sign was placed on Kakichi's house the keeper of the wineshop came to collect his account. He looked up at the small sign and laughed.

"Well, so it's true!" he mocked. "They told me you had become a Christian but I would not believe it. You, a son of Kokichi. And now a member of the Temperance Society, too! The people are laughing at that. It is all very well as an ideal perhaps, but if everyone were to agree with you, the tax on wine of two hundred and ten million yen would not be paid into the national treasury, and then the government would be in difficulties. You have forgotten, perhaps, that we sell wine for the sake of the country. However, that is all immaterial; I have come to collect the money you owe me."

And he drew out his bill. It was enormous, and Kakichi was obliged to say frankly that he had not the money with which to meet it at present.

"I thought not," the wine dealer continued in an aggravating manner. "But I thought, too, that maybe, if you would agree not to go on with this movement, it could easily be canceled," he suggested. "And of course it would scarcely be a recommendation for you if it were known how much you owe me for wine."

Kakichi's shoulders straightened; he raised his head. "It is not my bill, but I have said that I would pay it, and in time it will be paid. There can be no question of cancellation." And he went into his house.

The summer days passed rapidly now, and the time for the Bon Festival—the Feast of Lanterns, as it was called—was approaching. This was the season dedicated to the worship of departed spirits, a season which his mother carefully observed. Lanterns were hung on the porches and in the cemeteries to guide the spirits back to their former homes. Gifts were exchanged and a general holiday declared.

A letter came to Kakichi from his aunt and uncle in Gamagori suggesting that he come to them for this holiday. It was, they wrote, the height of the swimming season, and there was every reason to believe that he would enjoy a happy time with them. Yoshie joined her invitation to theirs.

Kakichi laid the letter aside with disappointment. There was nothing that would have afforded him more delight, but there was not the slightest possibility of such a visit. The small amount that he earned, and that derived from the sale of their silkworms, was necessary to maintain their food supply; there was, too, the wine bill to be paid. He wrote, simply, to thank them and regret that he could not come; there was sickness in his family and there was no extra money for journeys. He remembered with happiness the visit that he had enjoyed with them . . . but he could not come. Almost at once a letter arrived containing a money order, and the insistent request that part of this money go towards the family's expenses and the rest be used for his trip. Kakichi was overjoyed. He would not only see these people who were dear to him, and Yoshie too, but he would use this as an opportunity to visit Sasuke. That, he felt, was imperative. He bought a lantern for his mother, and some extra food besides the necessary potatoes and rice. He made a substantial payment on the bill at the wineshop. These things came first.

His mother had long desired this lantern, and there seemed to her now to be an especial reason for its use. A week before word had come to them of her daughter Asa's death, the official report of which Kakichi verified. Although this might have proved another blow of inestimable weight, Kakichi was surprised at the manner in which she viewed this new sorrow. At last her daughter was released from what must have been a most unhappy existence. The light of the lantern would guide her home.

Though its use was no part of his own beliefs now, he could not help but feel his mother's reverence for it as she hung the lantern prayerfully in front of her shop. It was graceful, diamond-shaped, and made of white wood pasted over with silvered paper, out of which had been cut the delicate figures of birds and angels. They looked, she said, as she ran her fingers gently over the figures of the angels, like her children. From the lantern she went to stand for a moment in meditative silence before the god-shelf. In the dim light of the flickering candles the pale blue smoke which came from the dark, pungent incense rose in two slender, unwavering columns to the low ceiling. Kakichi's eyes followed them prayerfully. If wisdom and might and the conviction of a God of love might descend upon these same graceful columns into the hearts of all Japanese men, the worship they afforded their ancestors might be transmuted into a deeper, surer beauty and service to the race of man.

And he made ready for his trip to Gamagori.

CHAPTER XII

A CRIMSON PURSE

KAKICHI HAD NEVER UNDERTAKEN A JOURNEY SO HAPPY AND free as was that short train ride from Upper Tsugu to the sea. Now he might sit for a moment, relaxed and with his hands folded, and think on many things. It might seem that conditions at home were no better, and yet to his mind they represented undoubted improvement. For one thing, he was no longer "overanxious," having learned to lean more steadily on divine strength and guidance, and to recognize its efficacy. His mother was more peaceful, too; Kokichi more gentle and submissive. Only Taiji, left almost completely to Yuriko's care when her mother was busy, still troubled him greatly. He turned all day restlessly upon his bed, still quite unable to walk, and unhappy for lack of amusement and interest.

Now, too, Kakichi could take Yoshie from the innermost places of his heart where, because of the press of circumstances, he had been forced to relegate her, unwilling to think of her too often. He could recall her anew in all her kindness and simplicity and loveliness. He could close his eyes and see her own, wide and bright and shining. He could plan all the countless things he would tell her, things stored up for this purpose alone; of Kakube-e, whom he had not seen for so long a while, but whom he remembered so vividly; of Mr. Murano, tall and dark and forceful, bending across his low desk each quiet Sunday evening to

speak in his clear, deep voice of the Christ to those few
who gathered to hear. And of the leper, looking now from
his bed, through the window, on sun and rain and the stars
of night and finding in these things an amazingly new
beauty. And of himself. He knew that in the manner customary in his country, his aunt and uncle hoped to affiance
him to Yoshie. He respected their love for him, and their
wish; these things touched him deeply. Ah, there was so
much to say to her! Yet all the words he planned to say, in
which his growing tenderness for her might be concealed,
were swept away when, stepping out upon the wide, sunny
platform at Gamagori, he confronted her.

He had helped out a stout old lady burdened with countless bundles and a superfluous amount of baggage, and for
a moment he stood confused in the midst of these things
hearing his name called in a woman's voice. He turned his
head.

"Kakichi! But, of course it *is* Kakichi, is it not?" And she
looked in surprise at the bundles all about his feet and the
puffing old lady following after.

"Your mother?" she asked respectfully. He stepped over
a big package quickly and stood before her in an instant,
his cap in his hand.

"No," he answered breathlessly, and looked down at her.

Oh, she was much prettier than he had remembered her
to be . . . much! Her dark hair was fixed so becomingly
in a modern style; her cheeks were smooth as old ivory and
delicately flushed as a flower. Her eyes were very bright.
But he could only look at her, forgetting all that he had so
carefully planned to say.

"Where were you going?" he asked confusedly.

"I came to meet you! Auntie told me the train. She said

something about your wanting to visit your brother, but she asked me to bring you back with me first."

They began to cross the bridge while she talked, leaving the old lady to the care of someone who had apparently come to meet her.

"It has happened just as I had hoped," Yoshie went on with suppressed excitement in her voice, and while Kakichi kept searching in his mind for some statement that might convey his own feelings. He could only experience the keen delight of her presence, and his very real joy in her sweetness and charm. He kept turning his head shyly to look at her, scarcely hearing her words.

"I came quite early, so as not to miss the train."

"Your hair is done differently," he said suddenly.

She laughed softly. "Yes. You look quite different, too, you know. At first, in that great crowd at the station, I was discouraged, thinking I might have missed you. You had a bandage on your head before, but you look different . . . somehow . . . I cannot explain, Kakichi. You even walk differently. But still, it is you, is it not?"

He walked closer to her side. She had on a bright summer kimono, with a gay pattern of delicately colored birds upon it, and a bright red sash. He felt as though she was his bride and his pride in her was great.

"It's a lovely dress," was all that he could say.

"Auntie made it for me. Tamako has one of the same pattern. But mine has the birds! There is a dance on the sixteenth; can you stay for it, Kakichi? We are all quite excited. And there's a theater party to-night, if you care to go. I've already bought tickets," she said shyly, taking a small purse made of bright red silk out of her sash.

He knew it was the custom for Japanese girls to do things of this nature, but he hesitated.

"You must not spend your money for me, Yoshie," he said suddenly, looking away quickly from the hurt in her lifted eyes. But in understanding of her gesture he closed his fingers gently about her own.

They walked very slowly, and Kakichi, whose eyes were accustomed to the mountains, looked out upon the beauty of the calm, wide sea. Far on the horizon an island lay like a thin, dark arm stretched into the blue. Nearer, another island, like half a gourd cut lengthwise, seemed to be floating on the surface of the water, breaking the tedium of the horizon with its vivid emerald green. It was ebb tide, and the little boats were pulled high upon the beach, their black hulls bleaching in the sun. Fishing nets hung like spread webs upon the white masts to dry.

It was a holiday season, so the curved blue bay was filled with boats, some with pennants of dark blue or white flying from their masts, while others were gayly decked with the flags of all nations. Kakichi, coming as he did from the sterner, poorer life of the mountains, was impressed with the richness and gayety displayed in this seacoast village. Yoshie had turned up the sandy path that led to his aunt's. He followed her and was almost immediately encompassed in the warmth of greeting.

Tama was there, and two of her friends, and their conversation, after they had delightedly welcomed him, centered about the play to which they were going. Kakichi, however, could not be persuaded to accompany them. He must rise early on the following morning to visit Sasuke. He wanted, also, to have an opportunity to talk to Yoshie before the following day, and intimated this desire to her. She gave her tickets to Tama, remaining behind with Kakichi, when early in the evening they all hurried away.

"Yoshie," he began directly, facing her on the small

porch, fragrant with flowers in the garden and the fresh, clean wind from the sea; "Yoshie, you are old enough now, I suppose, to have offers of marriage?" He swallowed nervously, watching her face anxiously all the while.

She hesitated. "My mother writes continually to say that there is an offer awaiting me at home. I have not answered it. I am undutiful, I expect, not to make a reply."

"No. No. I believe that one should be quite free in the matter of marriage."

She raised her head. "You believe that? It has not been so in our country, however," she reminded.

"I know. Many things that are new are coming into being to add to our growth. Things in which I believe." But, he thought, these things could be spoken of later. His hands were cold, his cheeks burning as with fever. Nevertheless, he plunged ahead.

"Yoshie, do you understand anything of the condition of affairs at my home?"

She hesitated again. "Auntie said there was illness."

"Yes, illness, and poverty too."

"My parents are poor," she answered him simply. "It is why I came here to work at the looms. I am acquainted with poverty."

"There is more. Do you know that my brother is in prison, accused of murder? In a small village these are important things to people outside one's family. We have that to struggle against." Her wide-open eyes never moved from his face.

"And that within a few months, sometime early this winter, I shall have to go away for army service, to be gone for two years?"

She leaned forward then. "What will your mother do,

Kakichi? How will they live, that sick father of yours and your brother?"

He shook his head. "There will be some way, Yoshie, but I cannot see it now."

She looked out across the small garden down to the dark line of the sea, the murmuring of which came to their ears softly, rhythmically.

"I can see a way. I shall come to help them."

"You! With my home as it is!"

"Because it is as it is, I would like to come."

"But, Yoshie." He got to his feet hurriedly. He *must* make her see! "It is not a happy home . . . such as this is . . . and with this freedom." He spread his arms wide. "I cannot marry now. I will not have you troubled and tied down, too, unable to care for you. But, when I come back . . . !"

When he came back! Ah, how long, how long that time seemed to him as he stood there, all his yearning for her crowding like a great pain in his breast, stifling the words he would say.

"When you come back," her low voice repeated. "And it is while you are gone that *they* will need me. Oh, Kakichi, let me come!"

"You are an angel sent from God, Yoshie," he said indistinctly, and his love for her stood in his eyes as he leaned towards her, tenderly, in the dusk.

He carried the sweetness of those precious moments with him when, the next morning, the gate of the prison swung open to him with a creak. The prison guard stood there with a pistol in his hand and looked at Kakichi closely. In all his life Kakichi had never before been subjected to such scrutiny. How could anyone, having stolen or killed, bear the gaze of those piercing eyes? It must be almost as intolerable as the burden of the knowledge of the crime itself. He shuddered. What miracle could release his brother from this dark place? What word could effect a new hope within him?

It was a considerable distance from the gate to the room where the prisoners awaiting trial were interviewed. He was given a brass ticket with a number on it and asked to wait. He waited . . . for three hours. There were others waiting with him, their faces white with fatigue and impatience. The time limit after which no interviews were allowed was gradually drawing nearer, and he had almost made up his mind that he would not be able to see his brother that day when the guard shouted his number.

He got to his feet quickly and followed another guard into the interviewing room, where those who came to see their friends talked through a small window with the prisoner. The window opened.

Kakichi caught sight of a narrow-eyed youth standing on the other side of the window in silence. His hair was brushed straight back, his face was heavy and sullen and utterly without color. He was clothed in the regulation prison garb of dark blue. Kakichi stared at him for a few seconds, unable to speak, and Sasuke did not open the thin, bitter line of his lips.

"Sasuke! How are you, Sasuke? Mother sent me to you, to bring her love and her prayers . . . all her best thoughts for you."

Sasuke raised a thin hand and ran it through his dark hair. A sudden tremendous wave of pity for this man swept Kakichi. He *would* say what was in his heart to say! And without any fear, now!

"I, too, pray to God each day for your deliverance," he began.

"Thanks," returned the other man dryly, "but that can

accomplish nothing. I'd rather that you gave me some money for tobacco." Kakichi felt as though he had been doused with cold water.

"I have already made arrangements with a shop to send you tobacco each day, and have left some money in the office for you to use as you please. I did not know how things were managed here, but they told me that that was the way in which it was done. I have a Bible here for you, too," and he put his hand inside his coat.

Sasuke laughed hoarsely. "A Bible! What would I want with a Bible, now? You can bring me a copy of Marx's works instead. I'm an atheist; I don't believe in such abstract things as God or spirit."

And he suddenly seemed to be violently excited. "I believe only in the perfection of the race through the abolition of capitalism," he proclaimed loudly.

"You are asleep, Sasuke, and while we sleep, as when we dream, we are only partly conscious. There may be other ways, too, in which the perfection of the race might be accomplished. You sleep," he repeated gently, "but it is not until we wake that we realize that we have been dreaming."

Sasuke ran his hand excitedly through his hair once more. "I don't understand what you are saying. I am fully awake. It is you who are passing the days in a dream, without real consciousness, deluded by a vision that can't be fulfilled. I am a martyr who has fallen for the sake of righteousness." And he beat his hands vehemently on the narrow shelf below the window and looked at his brother with a fixed stare in his narrow, black eyes.

Kakichi stared. "Sasuke, this is not the time for argument. We should not waste the moments in this fashion. Let us talk of other things."

"I know," Sasuke sneered. "You want to talk about your

religion. Well, I hate religion; I said all this to you once before and what I said I say again. It is the enemy of the masses; it is the opium that paralyzes the people. I cannot believe in it."

The guard stepped forward. "You have just one minute left," he cautioned them.

Kakichi's heart beat rapidly. One minute! So much to say and only one minute in which to say it! He wanted to urge his brother to open his mind and his heart, to approach the death sentence that he must most certainly face with a different spirit. To speak of these things would only infuriate Sasuke, and be unavailing. They would fall on ears that heard not. To speak of trivial things seemed equally futile.

Sasuke spoke again. "It is nothing to me, even if I do receive a sentence of death, for I do not believe that man has a soul. Death will kindly end everything."

"Oh no, brother, no!" Kakichi pressed forward impetuously. "The soul continues to exist even after death, and in the next world we will surely receive retribution for all undone in this present one. It is merely the effect growing from the cause . . ."

At that instant the wooden door which separated them dropped, leaving Kakichi staring at the barrier in a dazed manner. It had not been painted for years, and so many hands had touched it and had lifted it, that the paint was almost completely worn off. In the moment's bitter disappointment, it was this detail that caught his attention. How incongruous it was that just that narrow door should separate, as it were, one life from the next, one thought from the next. Why couldn't they have had a glass partition? Kakichi looked around. The walls, which had once been painted white, were marked with dirty fingerprints and scratched with nails; there was no relief of decoration or design anywhere. The whole place was bare and ugly, ugly in the extreme. He moved slowly towards the door, then stood quite still as he heard the clink of a saber on the far side of the partition, and then the flap-flap of straw sandals echoing on the cement floor as Sasuke was silently led away. Hot tears burned in his eyes as the sound of his brother's steps grew fainter, and with a silent commending of him into the hands of God, Kakichi left the prison.

He followed the shining tracks of the tramlines all the way back to Gamagori, trying to quiet the confusion of his thoughts. He had to go back to the mountains this same evening, but before he left he must see Yoshie once more.

She was waiting for him, and it seemed to him that the sight of her face made suddenly brighter the barren wastes of disappointment and grief within him. Assuredly her love and warm kindliness had illumined the desert places of his life.

They put on their bathing suits and went down to the wide, white sandy beach in front of his uncle Sadakichi's house, where a group of children were bathing in the surf. The tide was just at the full and the transparent sea covered the shoal shore like a moving mirror, and held the swimmers in its warm embrace. Yoshie, who had been born on these shores, was a skillful swimmer. Kakichi was always to remember her as she was that night, her slim figure cutting through the gently rippling waves. Her brown skin was refracted in the clear, blue sea water and blended with the white foam that curled up about her body as she swam, making to his eyes a picture of unsurpassed grace and beauty.

CHAPTER XIII

FAVORABLE AND OPPOSING WINDS

UPON KAKICHI'S RETURN HIS MOTHER WAS EAGER TO HEAR news of Sasuke, and Kakichi could say no more than that he was well, and seemingly without fear of his fate. What this must be there was no advantage in keeping from her; instinctively she knew the end that lay in store for him.

"And he sent us no message . . . no farewell?" she inquired, her faded eyes upon his face.

"His love, mother," Kakichi answered. She turned her head away slowly, making no reply. Perhaps, he thought sorrowfully, this was a futile lie; she did not believe him.

His absence, peculiarly enough, had been recorded in the village paper, and there had been included in the notice the information that Kakichi was interested in the promotion of temperance in the village. It had, in fact, spoken of him with commendation.

Kakichi was embarrassed. "Surely they must lack news, to have found me so important," he complained.

But his mother was not of the same mind. She was proud of the notice, she declared firmly.

"And besides," Yuriko added eagerly, "we had quite a few customers in the shop yesterday, people who came to ask about the society. And to buy things, too," she added happily.

But what interested Kakichi far more was that Mata, the miller, had called.

"Mata!" he exclaimed. "But what could he have wanted with me? They say he calls on no one."

"I do not know," his mother answered. "He said something about some mountain land in which he thought you might be interested."

Mountain land! Could it be possible that his dream of planting trees and raising new foodstuffs would be realized? He could hardly contain himself for curiosity and excitement. He had not long to wait, however, for Mr. Murano sought him out on the first evening that he was at home.

"I do not think I need to have come," the older man greeted him. "Your face looks as though you had already had all the good fortune you could possess."

"Still, tell me." Kakichi laughed happily.

"Well, Mata came to see me the other day; in some manner we talked about you. I had mentioned to him sometime ago your idea, and your hermit friend's, for cultivating the mountain areas, and he has become intensely interested. It appears that for a long time he has entertained similar ideas, dreamed the same dream. It is interesting, how these ideas seek each other out! He says that he has about six hundred acres of forest land that he would be glad to turn over to you to manage. He asked me to come in as a partner, too. What do you think of that?"

Kakichi's face was shining; there was no need for him to answer.

"He is a queer fellow in many respects, but he is reliable, and I don't think he would make false promises. Do you remember how we decided that Japan's imperative duty at this time was to love the land, to love her neighbors, and to love God? Well, Mata concurs with us in this belief; he believes, too, that in so far as it is possible we should put these ideas into instant practice, believes with us that there is need for them, not to-morrow, but to-day, and that post-ponement means disaster. Do you think you could manage this enterprise while you are working at the blacksmith's shop?"

"It must be managed, pastor," Kakichi said thoughtfully. "I cannot for the moment give up the one; it is our living. A decision between the importance of these two things will in some way be made for me. But I have always been in the mountains since I was quite young, and have a love for them. Still," he added, "I do not think I could care for six hundred acres all by myself." He paused a moment before continuing. "You know, I remember Kakube-e spoke about putting into practice agriculture in the third dimension. Cubic agriculture, he called it."

"Cubic agriculture?" Mr. Murano repeated curiously.

"Yes. I have thought about that term often, wondering just what he could have meant. I suppose one with a knowl-edge of God would interpret it as a trinity, a combination of forces under the soil and upon the earth's surface and above it, combined in all they signify to the imagination for growth and production. I think it must have been some-thing like this that he meant."

"I like that," Mr. Murano agreed warmly, after a mo-ment's thought. "I wish we could find this Kakube-e and bring him into our plans . . . although he is already in them, is he not?"

Kakichi nodded.

"Mata suggested that if it is practicable, it would be a good idea to form a group of ten or twelve young men in the two villages into a Land Improvement Association. He said that he would put all the profits from the mill into it for the first few years."

"And then," Kakichi added, "the next step would be a Producer's Co-operative Society."

Mr. Murano agreed. "Mata talked about it to Dr. Kurino, for he, too, owns some mountain land that is not at the moment arable. He has some ideas, too. And then there is my brother-in-law, who would probably join if the doctor and I would. He has one hundred and seventy acres. It promises to be a big piece of work, Kakichi. Some of this forest land has so far been used only for making charcoal, and won't be as ideal as we hope for, at all events, for a long time. However, with time and co-operation much can be done; look what has transpired in just a short time. If you include only the acres that belong to the Kurino family, you have twelve hundred, and that would necessitate the employment of a great many men every day for a long time. The common wood could be used for charcoal. And nut trees could be planted at once . . . of the sort that would flourish. Chestnuts and apricots could be grown!" He broke off short, laughing at his own enthusiasm as the prospect grew and grew. In the end they both set off to talk it over with Mata; they could not wait.

He lived below the mill in a brown house nestled on the bank of the Lower Tsugu River. Its windows looked out above the trees to the waters below. He lived a somewhat isolated life; the whole air of the place was one of marked tranquillity. He read and studied a great deal, Mr. Murano told Kakichi. He was, although it was not well known, a graduate of the Tokyo Agricultural College, and an authority on the subject of industrial co-operation.

He was at home, as they expected, and they were soon in earnest conversation.

"The land is all idle," he was saying, "and it is time that it be utilized. It needed only this! If we can get a harvest of nutritious foodstuffs, starches, carbohydrates and fats, and the people will eat them, and feed the oversupply to the pigs, those who live in the mountains will be quite self-supporting, and there will be no famine in our land. We can get hams and bacon from the pigs, and if in addition we keep goats and drink the milk, Japan need not be troubled for a long time to come over the food supply. There is still plenty of unused land to be opened up."

These were, Kakichi said in pleased surprise, ideas similar to those of Kakube-e's, and which he had, until now, merely glimpsed.

"The Japanese treat their land too carelessly," Mr. Murano interjected. "They waste what is given them for use. We ought at least to do as they do in Germany, and plant even the smallest piece of ground with infinite care. When you compare the area of Japan with that of England, we have far more land; there is no reason why we should not be able to feed double our population. There are about two hundred and six people to the square mile in Japan while, I have read, there are about three hundred and seventy-five to the square mile in England."

Kakichi listened with keen interest to this conversation, while Mata continued:

"The young people of the farms and villages have never been taught co-operation; it is no wonder their farming is unprofitable. Industry makes profits because it has a large amount of capital to invest, it has huge and modern machines, it has organized its work by division of labor. Its purpose is more united, its profits more sure. And still the people starve for bread. Electric power could be brought into these mountain villages through the acquiring of capital in an association set up for land . . . and not just manufacturing . . . improvement, believing that out of this all the rest would follow. With the power we could not only employ electric lighting, but carry on lumbering and milling, from hulling grain to making flour, with greater expediency, so that the village would prosper. We could, if everyone became a member, redistribute the arable land and straighten out our curving, oft-disputed boundary lines. Not only would the land improve and tenancy rates go down, but there would be an abundance of labor for those not employed, and countless side-line occupations would be developed and stimulated. As the working up of agricultural products would increase, the manufacture of foodstuffs would likewise develop. We would learn how to make and cure hams and bacons, and how to use nuts, fruits, dried figs, raisins, and foods made from goats' milk. The farming villages would be lifted out of their continual poverty."

"Into a more abundant life," Kakichi said enthusiastically, seeing the dream unfold. Mr. Murano nodded.

"There are more changes and advantages in our planning than can be, for the moment, counted up," he said thoughtfully.

Kakichi understood clearly what an agricultural co-operative might mean, from the glimpse he had had of the Silk Co-operative business on his trip with Kakube-e but he could not visualize such an ideal community developing immediately in the village in its present condition. He could but see the first steps, and dream of those to follow, and Mr. Murano assured him that this, for the moment, was enough. But he listened none the less to all that Mata was propounding. Who could have guessed that he . . . a landholder and man of wealth . . . held these theories?

"If the villages would co-operate, we could easily carry on even such an enterprise as co-operative silk manufacture, and put our girls to work in that. We could also manage warehouses for agricultural products, and our credit associations, instead of being the poorly organized institutions they are now, could be developed into dependable organizations. Our daily necessities could be purchased through a co-operative, and the vegetable fertilizer that is so necessary to the land could be obtained in the agricultural laboratory at Oharo. Co-operatives might even be formed so that, if a family has widespread illness, their land would be cared for and their crops protected, and the family would not be so utterly overwhelmed by their trouble, as is often the case now. Under conditions such as these life would be much easier and much more pleasant in a village than in the city, and our young people would not be so easily attracted in that direction, nor driven there for lack of some sustaining occupation. The farming villages would be able to maintain three or four times their present population.

"Oh, I have had these ideas for a long time; I have read and studied and made countless inquiries as to the economic benefits to be derived from some such plan. Certainly the situation is drastically in need of some remedy. But when I have suggested anything of a similar nature the people only laughed and contented themselves with the reminder that I was a queer sort of person. They have all been self-centered and have lacked the essential elements for a change of any kind. And there has been no one who could assume leadership. I think you can do this, Kakichi, and you are young enough and becoming well known enough to attract other young people to such an enterprise. We need their fervor and their young enthusiasm, their young ideals."

Mata took several ten-yen bills from his girdle and handed them to Kakichi.

"I think it would be a good plan if you and I went together to look over some of this mountain land for two or three days. This will take care of your family's expenses while you are away and recompense you for any time you may lose at your work. And hereafter, whenever you are away on similar errands, I will see that you receive compensation for your time."

"But," objected Kakichi, overwhelmed at this sudden kindness, "it is far too much, sir. I could not accept . . ."

Mata thrust the bills into his hand. "You will have to accept it," he maintained. "It is the only condition under which I will turn over my lands."

As Pastor Murano and Kakichi left the house, and followed along the high green hedge which had been planted around the garden at the rear, Mr. Murano, his face radiant with smiles, remarked, "And they call him a queer sort of chap!"

"Well," said Kakichi warmly, drawing a deep breath, "I believe I approve of that kind of queerness."

CHAPTER XIV

An Angel Weaving at a Loom

THERE WAS NOW ANOTHER, AND MORE PERSONAL PROBLEM OF Kakichi's, to be considered. While the first steps were being taken in this new co-operative plan, Kakichi felt that he must discuss the possible arrival of Yoshie with his mother. A letter had come from Yoshie one morning several days after the conversation with Mata, and in it she said that if she secured her father's permission she would come to Upper Tsugu within a few days. She wanted to go on earning money with her weaving, and she asked if they had a loom at which she might work.

Yoshie's name had only been mentioned in the most casual conversation, including Kakichi's uncle and aunt and their many friends, and Kakichi felt that it was time for his mother now to know more about the girl.

Masa was out, having gone to cut off the water from flowing into their rice field, which had also been rented through the kindness of Mata. She did not notice Kakichi when he came out from the side of the mill, for she was busy cutting the drain that would divert the water. He approached her hesitantly, not sure how to begin.

"I can do that for you, mother," he said, and took the hoe from her hand.

She looked up, surprised. "What are you doing here at this time of day?" she wanted to know. "Aren't you working at the forge?" Her tone was anxious.

"No. I came to talk with you about something."

"You are going into the service . . . now . . . sooner?" she asked quickly, but he smiled reassuringly and watched the frightened expression disappear from her eyes. But his heart was beating rapidly; she might be opposed to all he had to suggest.

"No; nothing like that. It is only that when I was at Gamagori a friend of my aunt's said that she would like to come and live with you and help you when I am away on conscription. And she has written to say that she may come very soon."

As he spoke he opened a wide cut in the dike which had been made thick and strong, and the water, which had formed a shallow pond outside the fields, now began to flow gently to the lower level with a soft, rushing sound. Kakichi watched the stream carefully, listening all the while for her answer.

"But that's very nice," she said at length. "But there's no fit place for her to sleep, is there?"

"I told her that, and she says she will sleep in the front of the shop . . . or anywhere. It was . . ." He stopped in embarrassment, but when he raised his eyes she was laughing.

"She is really a very nice girl," he began again. "You shall see, mother," he promised, feeling his face flush.

"Oh, of that I am sure, my son," she said gently. "And it is perhaps your aunt's idea that this girl should be your wife?"

"Well, I suppose it is something like that," he admitted, with a laugh.

"Well, that's fine! If she is a good girl, who will come to a house as poor as ours and where there is sickness, and you are pleased with her, we had better have her come right away, hadn't we?"

"May I write, then, to say that she may come?" he asked eagerly, looking earnestly into his mother's smiling face.

She nodded, and he went back to the shop happily, singing the song he had once sung when . . . oh, how long ago it all seemed now . . . when he had worked on the banks of the river, drawing the logs to the shore.

Less than a week later a letter came saying that Yoshie's father and mother had seen the short article in the paper about Kakichi and the Temperance Society, and had given their consent to her going to his home as an affianced bride. She said that his aunt had also visited her home, and that her parents were apparently well satisfied. She would be arriving within a few days, and she asked that they set up a loom somewhere . . . anywhere . . . at which she might work.

Kakichi consulted his mother about the loom, and she suggested that if they asked Mr. Murano he might know of one, which he did. He remembered that there were several of an old-fashioned type which had been discarded and put away in the corner of the storehouse at the old Kurino homestead, and he went there to find that they would gladly give one of them. Kakichi's little house was crowded, and it was a problem for the moment where to put it, but they finally decided on a place on the south side of the kitchen, in the courtyard, against the wall and sheltered from the rain by the wide, projecting brown eaves of the roof.

There could be, of course, no great preparations made for Yoshie's arrival; nevertheless, the whole atmosphere of the small house was charged with a new and happy excitement. Even Kakichi seemed brighter as he listened to Taiji's excited conjectures as to what Yoshie might be like. Masa could only look at Kakichi and smile happily at his own happy countenance.

Yoshie arrived two days later, in the midst of a pouring rain. In her arms she carried her clothes, neatly wrapped in the usual square cloth bundle. It was impossible to describe Kakichi's joy at sight of her, a joy augmented when he saw that his mother, over whom he had worried most, was apparently instantly fond of her. There was something in the nature of a blessing in the fact that Yoshie was to live under the same roof with him and his family. He was warmed by the knowledge of her gentle presence, and followed her about with his eyes.

She seemed to fit at once into the simple routine of their life. He marveled at the ease with which she adjusted herself, and as the days passed he became increasingly aware of her presence there, a presence always more felt than seen. She became an almost invisible factor for good, and the service she contributed was immeasurable, and yet never was it rendered in any way that commanded either attention or expected commendation or that took from Kakichi's mother her rightful position in that house.

It was Yoshie who carried the meals to Kokichi and Taiji, bringing with them a great deal more than the meals, for cheerfulness of mien was sadly needed in that household. It was Yoshie who rose in the morning and, while Kakichi built the fire, prepared the rice for boiling and saw that the bean soup was made ready for the day. In innumerable ways she contrived to lift from Masa's shoulders the many things that she had been called upon to do, so that her service was loving and tender and thoughtful in the extreme. She helped in the rice fields, and in her spare time she worked at the loom. There was no place in the village where she could secure the necessary materials for weaving silk, so she wove cheap cotton cloth instead. It was market-able in the village, and brought in a meager reward for her work.

At night she slept in a narrow space in the store, as any maid would do, and this was a situation to which Kakichi's mother uttered instant objection, but which Yoshie gently but firmly overruled. No one in that household was to give up his or her place to her. Her position in the house was to remain no more than that of a servant until Kakichi re-turned from the service and they would be married. His mother was more than surprised at this decision but Kakichi maintained that they had again discussed it and thought it best to leave their marriage until that later day, when he would feel more free to marry.

So she did not go around to the neighbors to introduce this bride, so different from the ordinary brides that came to the village, as was the custom. They went only to Totaro's house next door.

Yoshie went with Kakichi to the evening services on Sun-day. It was her wish, and Kakichi was overjoyed at it.

"Well, you see," she explained shyly, "your interest in it has led me to ask questions, too, Kakichi. There is so much I would learn, in order to be a Christian. You know so much more about it than I do."

And he could only look at her tenderly. How could knowledge be measured if not by service? And surely there was no one who would not declare Yoshie's life and service to be Christlike.

So the weeks passed into months, passed rapidly because they were happy, happy despite the fact that as the day for military service drew near Kakichi grew more and more anxious. He was leaving so much work undone, so much still to be accomplished. He had with some difficulty been able to start the village Temperance Society, and both he and Mr. Murano were gratified with the new members and the plans made for procedure. The Land Improvement Association, even with Mata's assistance, had not yet come into being. They had no more than the bare outlines for it, although he and Mata had gone, early in September, to look at the forest land and had found it to be most promising. Then they had approached the school principal, Toyama, who was likewise the president of a Young Men's Association of the village, soliciting his support of their plan. They asked if he could suggest any young men of ability and character, men in need of employment, but he was doubtful and hesitant.

"This is all a very brilliant idea," he told them agreeably, "but you cannot expect the young men of this village to work on farms. All men of any ability or ambition go to the cities."

"And they starve in the cities," Kakichi remonstrated, "and fall into bad habits and . . ."

"Even so, those who remain here are those who are kept for some reason and cannot go away. They starve on the farms, too. They have no interest in the mountains."

"That is admitted," Kakichi interposed. "And it is our plan to stimulate such an interest."

"It's a big undertaking," was Toyama's pessimistic rejoinder.

This was, as they found in the succeeding days, only too true. It was an exaggeration to say that there were no steady young men in the village, nor some men whose imaginations were not kindled by the proposed plan, but they were pitifully few, and it was clearly evident that they would need active leadership. It was then that Kakichi realized that there was something fundamentally wrong with the education in his country, and possibly in other lands as well. Up to the present time it had been an education that trained officials, or salaried men, but it was not one which taught men love of the land, of mankind, of God. It was an education that trained boys to go to the city to become men of fame and position, goals at which they failed more often than not, living in incredibly crowded conditions while the villages remained deserted and farms lapsed into ruin, and there was no inducement to return to them. Those who died each year from starvation died in vain; something drastic must remedy the situation. He made up his mind then that even if he and Yoshie were the only ones to do it, they would begin by planting a few trees and raising something besides rice. But before he had time to go any further with these plans, he was put into jail.

An article appeared in the paper disclosing the fact that he, a professed believer in the Christian faith, which faith was harming the spirit of the country and laying waste all its established beliefs and customs, had as an elder brother a man who was not only an avowed communist but a convicted murderer. It was known that he, Kakichi, was instrumental in propounding extremely socialistic ideas in the village, ideas which might prove injurious to the welfare of the same.

Kakichi was aghast at this bitter accusation, and his mother wrung her hands in despair. Mr. Murano was away, and before Kakichi could seek Mata's advice on this new state of affairs, his instant appearance was requested at the Taguchi police station. The charges were so preposterous and the whole thing in fact so unexpected that Kakichi was at a loss for adequate defense.

"What's this now, young man?" the official demanded sternly. "Your family has already caused us sufficient trouble, it would seem, without this charge against you. According to the opinion of the school principal, Mr. Toyama, you are attempting to put into practice ideas that would injure the rights of landowners, and enable tenants to profit at their expense. Have you, too, gone radical through the influence of your worthless brother? It is the intention of this government to suppress all such activities as you propose."

Kakichi opened his mouth to reply. It was inconceivable that men of this man's supposed intelligence would mistake love for force, and confuse a co-operative enterprise with work done for the advantage of any one class!

"And furthermore," pursued the man disagreeably, "they say you have brought your sweetheart to live in your house, and contrary to all established custom have made no immediate plans for your wedding. Is this true? She is one of your group, too, I suppose?"

Kakichi had no spirit with which to enter into an argument upon these things, but he knew with a sudden fear that Yoshie might be not only misjudged but mistreated, and that, he felt, he could not permit. It was best to be silent. Those who knew him would believe in him. It was futile to attempt even the partial explanation which it was probable would be all that would be allowed him. One thing, however, was clear. It was apparently Toyama who had reported that he was plotting to convert the village over to socialistic principles. If his cause would prosper, those who could adequately defend him would be summoned to that defense.

So his imperturbability was interpreted as hardness and his quiet manner as insolence, and he was locked up without further examination. In his cell he realized that such misunderstanding was to be expected. In view of his family's reputation, his new activities would naturally arouse the suspicions of people who did not know him well. But there were a few who understood him and were at one with him, and their understanding and belief would effect his release. He would wait, and fill his waiting with a hopeful, prayerful expectancy.

On the next day the examination was continued. They asked him for a list of the members of his group and he steadily maintained that no group had yet been formed. When this examination had been repeated for several days, he was released because they could bring no positive charge against him. He returned home to find that both Yoshie and Mr. Murano had made repeated trips to Taguchi to see him but had been denied admittance as well as the privilege of sending him a message of any kind. He found, too, that, according to information gained by the blacksmith's wife, his name had been taken off the list of members of the Young Men's Association. Even Pastor Murano was utterly astonished at the strange turn affairs had taken, but counseled Kakichi not to be discouraged, there was surely something for good in this upheaval. One could not always at the moment see all the road lying ahead, and if it was concealed, it was concealed for some purpose in which God had a part.

But Kakichi's chief concern, and Yoshie's too, since she was vitally interested, was over the disappearance of the leper and his children. That they had been driven from the shed was obvious, and no one knew where they had gone. They searched at every opportunity for trace of them, but it seemed unavailing.

On his return home Kakichi had been warned by the police: "You had better be careful hereafter, and conform to the life of this community. If you deliberately form a

secret association without permission, the Chief of Police
will issue orders for your arrest. He says that whether you
call it a Land Improvement Co-operative Association or a
Forest Improvement Association, it will make no difference;
after all, these are nothing but means for propagating
radical ideas that disturb the peace of the village."

Kakichi well understood, when he received this warning,
how wildly misunderstandings spread, but to him it came
as an invitation to redouble his efforts towards establishing
benefits that could be recognized and not misinterpreted.
His service, he knew, was not mercenary nor limited to the
advantage of any one group. It was that anyone who wished
might partake of its benefits and have bread enough to eat.

In the midst of these difficulties the only ones who never
had doubted him were the eccentric landowner, Mata, Dr.
Kurino and Mr. Murano. And, Kakichi felt rightly, these
men represented the highest type in the village, so that he
could be justifiably proud of their co-operation. They were
honest Christian men.

And of course there were Yoshie and his mother; their
faith never wavered.

In evidence of his belief in their plans and in Kakichi,
Mata went to the city of Nagoya and ordered five thousand
seedlings of various kinds, among them chestnut, walnut,
apricot and cypress. And that autumn, as the winds tore the
broad leaves from the trees of the Tsugu mountains and
carpeted the winding roads with their bright beauty,
Kakichi and Mata and Yoshie would start out, over these
roads, by the fading light of the morning stars, and would
work at clearing away the common underbrush on Mata's
lands. Kakichi gave up his work at the forge to do this, and
so they laid their plans for planting a forest, the products
of which could be utilized.

Their efforts were not in vain. By the middle of December, with Yoshie's assistance, they had planted twenty-five acres. And it was understood that when Kakichi went into the service, Yoshie and Mata would go on with the work.

Towards the end of that month the condition of Kakichi's father grew steadily worse, so that there were days when Kakichi was obliged to stay at home to nurse him instead of going to the mountains. On one of these days, while he was busy in the shop, two beggar children came and looked in at the window. On looking at them more closely he recognized them as the children of the leper. He opened the door quickly.

"Why, Chokichi!" he addressed the older one. "Where have you gone to? We have looked for you for many weeks."

The children led him to a shed many miles below the village. It was a most horrible place and had once been used for storing manure. It had no roof and no floor save the cold, damp earth. They had no quilts and no furniture of any kind. How they had managed to survive was beyond his imagination. They could not remain here throughout the winter months. He thought suddenly of the hermit's cave deep in the mountains, where Kakube-e had lived and where, for all he knew, he might even now be living. If there were only a cave like that in which to house these destitute people! He set out to look, and Yoshie went with him.

"They are what Christ must have meant when he spoke of the 'least of these,' and what they will do when I am away I do not know."

"But you *do* know!" Yoshie spoke with certainty. "Am I not here to be your hand, your foot, your eye?"

And his hand held fast to hers in a deep, inexpressible

joy. Surely, God was good to have made evident to him such
a perfect love!

There were caves. They found any number of them on
either side of the road that ran up through the mountains,
caves that had once been used for storing silk-worm eggs.
They were dry and comparatively warm, and some of them
had two openings, one of which could be made into a kind
of window. Yoshie assured him that they could be made
livable; they would serve until something better could be
found. So, Kakichi carried the leper on his back, and
Yoshie drew a cart with their few poor belongings. They
brought quilts and some cooking utensils and established
them here in the hills.

The sick man could do no more than put his thin hands
together in an attitude of worship as he watched them both.

"I will have to go away soon," Kakichi told him gently,
"but you need not be anxious, for this girl will come daily
to care for you. And this time we will tell no one but the
doctor and Mr. Murano where you are."

On the fifth day of January Kakichi received his notice
for departure on the following day, and his mother and
Yoshie hurried in their final preparations for him.

There were five of them to go into the service from
Upper Tsugu, and these, with the seven from the lower
village, were all required to leave at the same time. It was
the custom on such occasions for the people to go to the
village boundary to see them off. It was also the custom to
put up banners in front of the doors of those going into
service, banners contributed by friends and relatives, and
bearing congratulatory inscriptions and phrases. There were
no banners in front of Kakichi's house, and of course there
were only his mother and Yuriko and Yoshie to bid him
farewell at the edge of the village. These outer evidences

might all seem to be lacking, but inwardly Kakichi had been supplied with all he might need. Mr. Murano had come on the previous day to say his farewell, to assure Kakichi of his constant thought and prayer, and to bless him. Mata had come too, although he hated excitement of such a nature. He had brought with him a package of books for Kakichi, with the suggestion that he might find time for them, and Kakichi had taken them gratefully, eagerly.

So there were no banners and no cheers, and only his mother's tearstained, anxious face, and Yoshie's sweet, pale one. Yuriko was too childishly excited to elicit great concern although Taiji had been loud in tearful remonstrances at his brother's departure.

"I shall miss you," he wailed cheerlessly, and Kokichi nodded in mute confirmation of the boy's statement.

"But if I hadn't gone, Yoshie would not have come to you," Kakichi sought to remind them. There was so much he wanted to say to her alone, but words were futile and he could only enfold her gently in his arms and speak her name tenderly before they parted.

At the village edge, the recruits were to get into a bus, and now there was no question as to whether one had many banners or few or none at all. It seemed, in fact, as though the greater the number of banners the more they were in the way. There was dreadful noise and confusion and everyone shouted farewells, and the next moment the bus, with a roar from its noisy engine, started down the mountain road to the south. In the press of the crowd Kakichi could not even turn his head to look back. But the memory of the loving faces behind him, and the loving hearts who held him close in their thoughts, went with him all the way.

CHAPTER XV

ORION AT DAWN

IT WAS A BITTERLY COLD WINTER. THERE WERE ICICLES FIVE
inches long hanging from the end of the roof gutters, and
the snow that had fallen early in the month lay unmelted
for weeks under the eaves on the north side of the house.
Yoshie, who had been accustomed to spending the winter
in a warm place like Gamagori, where the sea winds seemed
to temper the climate, felt the cold keenly on this high
plateau two thousand feet above the sea. Her hands and
face were chapped and sore, and her clothing seemed insufficient to keep her warm. At night she shivered and coughed
and was chilled by the fear that she might be ill. That,
surely, must not happen. There were too many things to be
done and her joy in doing them was so real. Though
Kakichi was not there and she missed him dreadfully, as
indeed they all did, life in the little house went on smoothly.
It began steadily to bear the imprint of her care and
thought; in every aspect it testified to a simple but evident
neatness and care. Life was easier for them all.

In the morning when the fire was built in the stove, she
would find the water which she had drawn the night before
frozen in the wooden bucket, and when she went to the
stream she had to break the ice to reach the clear, running
waters beneath. She loved to stand there, as Kakichi used
to stand in the early morning, and gather her thoughts into
quietude for the day. It was a moment for consecration. In

the distance the mill wheel turned with a low rumble, and the cocks crowed here and there as they greeted the dawn. The woods were still deep in a dark, drowsy quiet, as though not fully awakened from their dreams; it was still too dark to distinguish the tip of one branch from another. The sky above, hemmed between the dark peaks of the mountains, was sprinkled with pale stars like the dust of silver, dissolving in the first tints of the dawn. And, brightest among them was Orion, to which she raised her eyes with the thought that somewhere Kakichi might rise too, in the early morning, to look upon its beauty and its brightness, and seek in it the symbol for the day at hand. She would pray silently to the God to whom he prayed, a God whose meaning had expanded joyously with the added definition this new life here had brought to her. She would place into His hands the fortunes of this family with whom she had come to live, and the safety and welfare of Kakichi himself, with whom she felt such a complete oneness, and ask that her own efforts might continue with strength and inspiration throughout the day.

After that, the day's tasks really began. There was cooking and baking and cleaning, and all of this routine was undertaken with a cheerfulness of mien and a happiness that became infectious. Even Kokichi found means to express his gratification, and his satisfaction with the good things she managed to prepare for him to eat. As for Yuriko and Taiji, they frankly and openly adored her. To Taiji, especially, she was as light come into the darkness and dreariness of his days. She always knew stories to tell, bringing up from her young, imaginative mind a wealth of new thought for him to dwell upon. She found things for his hands to do, new ways of making him comfortable. On days when it was too cold to go into the woods for the planting which she continued so zealously there was weaving and sewing. Kakichi's mother marveled continually at her industry and her skill, marveled at the new peace that had come to her house. She herself worked long and faithfully, but Yoshie had managed to take from her shoulders the heaviest burdens, and she rubbed those same shoulders gently when they became stiff and lame. Masa assumed a loving and protective attitude towards her, and found small ways of expressing this love and gratitude. When Yoshie was chilled and tired, and came in from visiting the leper or from the hills, there was a fresh slice of hot rice cake for her toasted over the charcoal fire, or a sweet potato roasted in the ashes, or, more rarely, a cup of strong, hot tea.

Yuriko, too, sought for ways in which to help and show her attachment to Yoshie. She loved to sleep with her, bringing to the girl a grateful warmth and friendliness. She threaded her weaver's reed and rewound the woof thread on the reels; she helped in the making of thongs for wooden clogs which they sold in the village, a supplementary occupation that added to their tiny revenue throughout the winter months. During the three days of the New Year's holiday, which was all Yoshie could be persuaded to take, although Masa was very insistent that she needed a rest, she made a new sleeping garment for Kokichi, and a new dress for Yuriko. The child was delighted with this; it had been a long while, indeed, since she had had a new dress. It was made from a dress of Yoshie's, one she had never worn and that had been a gift wrapped carefully in a white cloth for future use. It was silk and had a bright, gay pattern, and Yuriko, who had never had a silk dress nor one half so pretty, ran her fingers lovingly over its soft folds, and when it was finished she stood before the mirror on which the quicksilver was cracked and worn, so that the image of her figure was distorted, and peered at herself delightedly.

"I shall wear it when Kakichi comes home," she said happily, "and for your wedding, Yoshie. Do you think I could wear it before that, perhaps? It seems so long to wait."

Yoshie looked at the child gravely, affectionately. Yes, long indeed. The longing pulled tightly at her breast; in order to release it she must give joy to someone. She smiled. "We must find a time sooner than that," she promised.

Taiji looked at his sister and could not keep silent. His heart had grown as sad as his small body, so that his hopelessness stood in his eyes. "Yoshie," he asked, "is there nothing that could be made for me?"

"Let's think! What could I make for you, Taiji?" she asked gently. She could not imagine what she could do for this child. His plight lay so heavily upon her heart; her wish to help him was so insistent. Yet Dr. Kurino insisted that they were doing all they could. For his body, perhaps, yes.

"I wish I could have a silk kimono. I have never had one," he told her.

"Why, Taiji," Yuriko chided. "If you were to have one to wear, where would you wear it? In bed?"

"I would go to the theater in the village to see a play. It is very tiresome lying in bed, and I often pretend that I go to the village. I'd put on my silk kimono and have a girdle of silk."

"To the theater?" Yoshie repeated.

"Sometimes there are children's plays at the theater," he told her.

"*The Forty-seven Ronin* is there now," Yuriko interrupted. "But *how* could you go?"

He looked at her thoughtfully, his dark eyes widening. "Well, you might carry me on your back as mothers do their babies," he suggested timidly. Yoshie raised her head suddenly to look at them both.

"No. You are too heavy for that. But I could carry you easily," she said suddenly, wondering why she had never thought of that before.

There began, then, an excited search through the household's possessions for something with which to make Taiji a kimono. But the surplus materials had long since been used up, and nothing could be found. Taiji, his dream having become so perfect and so real a thing, wept despairingly.

While Yoshie worked at her loom, he pondered over this situation. The play began to assume a tremendous significance. He *must* go!

"Yuriko," he called suddenly to his sister in the next room. She came to him obediently. "Yuriko, could you bring Yoshie's clothes in here so that I might see them. Perhaps she has something I might wear."

The girl protested stolidly. "She would have given it to you, Taiji. We can't go through her things. Besides, she hasn't anything, I'm sure."

"But couldn't we look?" he begged. Yuriko heard the lively sound of Yoshie's shuttle belowstairs. "Please," he persisted.

Well, he was sick, and there would be nothing. Yuriko brought the neatly wrapped bundle to Taiji's bed. Kokichi looked on disapprovingly. Taiji raised himself eagerly on his elbow. There were, indeed, pitifully few possessions, and only those to which they had become accustomed through seeing her wear them. But, wrapped carefully in some folds of soft paper, they found a beautifully broad-striped, deep blue coat. They looked at it with wide, bright eyes, and touched it with careful, loving fingers.

"It would make a beautiful kimono," Taiji breathed wistfully, but Yuriko wrapped it up quickly and carefully, almost reverently. "You couldn't take that, Taiji," she said firmly, remembering its lovely blue. "It's too beautiful. And it must be a very valuable coat; she has wrapped it so carefully." And Taiji turned his face away from the sight of her and was silent.

Only a few moments after Yuriko had put the things away where she had found them, Yoshie came up the stairs and into the room. Her eyes were bright and she smiled at them as if she knew a secret. They held their breaths. From behind her back she drew the blue coat!

"As I was weaving I thought of this. How would you like to have a kimono made from this coat?" Taiji and Yuriko, and Kokichi too, the latter with tears in his eyes, stared at her without speaking.

"You wouldn't really cut that beautiful coat?" Yuriko managed to ask.

"Don't you think it would make a beautiful kimono, too? And I have no need for it," she assured them cheerfully. "Taiji has. I think his need is quite important." But Yuriko still laid a protesting hand upon her arm.

"Did you make it?"

Yoshie nodded, her bright eyes on the coat.

"You made it for your marriage to Kakichi?"

"But I shan't need a coat, I'm sure," she said, and began to rip out the sleeve, while they watched her humbly and said nothing.

On the night when it was finished Yoshie put the kimono

on him, making of this a great occasion. Then she took
him on her back, with a hooded garment thrown over them
both, and they went down into the village. Yuriko could
not be left behind, of course, and besides, this was a welcome opportunity to wear the new dress. Yoshie had contrived to get enough money to pay for their entrance, but
there was not enough to supply them with seats, so that
they were obliged to stand in the gallery until the final act
at eleven o'clock. People stared at them curiously, especially
between the acts when Yoshie was obliged to go outdoors
with the children for a breath of fresh air. Her back ached
painfully, but the children were so delighted and happy
with the play that she could not bear to leave before it
was over.

How they talked about that play, afterwards . . . for
days and days . . . how they planned new plays, such as
they might write. Yoshie listened to them, happily, marveling at the new light of interest in their eyes. But, even more
than supplying them with this happiness, it suggested to
Yoshie something to do for Taiji, something that was to
lead to wider results.

As the winter days advanced and the ice melted and the
snow disappeared, she went more regularly to her work
on the mountains, going sometimes with Mata to plant the
seedlings, but more often alone. And when the distance was
not too great, she strapped Taiji to her back, carrying him
with her all the way, and putting him down under some
tree where they might talk and he could watch while she
worked. How he loved these expeditions, and the improvement in his health was simply astonishing. It was on one
of these days that he made his first attempt to walk. It was
a poor and stumbling attempt . . . but there was no one

to see if he failed. Yoshie's prayers were raised above the very hilltops for him, for she saw, she knew. Together they planned how, one day, he would surprise his mother, and Yoshie would set him down in the garden, and he would walk for her delight. With the passing days the dream became more and more of a reality, so firmly were their thoughts fixed upon it.

Yoshie read and reread Kakichi's letters, writing to him as often as she could, breathing out to him in her letters her love and her hopes, attempting to show him through the poor medium of words Taiji's desire, his mother's patience, and Yuriko's loving industry. But there was so little time in which to write; her letters were of necessity short. There was the leper . . . there was the planting . . . all of these dreams of Kakichi in which she had been given a part, and for the continuance of which she had been brought here. It was some greater will than her own that possessed her, some strength beyond her own that endured, some love of which she had become the pure exponent. And when, in the spring, she was taken suddenly ill and could not sleep at night because she was so chilled, nor during the day because her body burned with fever, not all of Masa's tenderness, nor Dr. Kurino's kindly words and the medicines he gave her, could comfort her. She was impatient to be up and working; this sickness was unfaithfulness to her trust. She could not, she dared not, be ill. Her tremendous determination to continue brought her to her feet long before she should have been about again.

Once more the house was quiet and orderly and there was about it an air of accomplishment. The shop prospered, too, and even Kokichi, who knew his days to be numbered, was at peace.

So the summer passed, and the autumn and the early days of the next winter, and there was no day on which Yoshie's spinning wheel was silent or her work undone, nor one on which she did not give the result of these labors into God's keeping.

CHAPTER XVI

THREE O'CLOCK IN THE MORNING

IN THE MEANTIME, KAKICHI ADJUSTED HIMSELF AS RAPIDLY as possible to the life of a soldier. By the time the first winter's snows had melted, he began to feel that this new discipline was not such an unwelcome thing. He felt that under it, with a proper realization of guidance, men might develop characteristics of tremendous value. Obedience and order were necessary adjuncts not to be despised, and those men who rebelled most readily were those, he found, whom he might have envied in the village, sons of wealthy men and used to ease. The food that to them was poor was better than any he had had at home. The beds were clean and not as hard to his young body as to theirs. He was better equipped, he found, in more ways than one, for endurance. The guns at whose heaviness they protested so bitterly were less heavy than a blacksmith's hammer, and much lighter than the logs he had dragged from the river waters. There was something here, too, that his life in the village had not afforded—leisure. And in this leisure time Kakichi began to study, remembering the man who had visited Mr. Murano's. He crowded into every rare, free hour all the learning he could imbibe, using Mata's gift of books avidly, gratefully. He read about government and farming. He read philosophy and social ethics. He read and reread and hungered for more. Each page was a new channel which he might explore. And there was, first and foremost, the Bible, with which he became in these days increasingly familiar.

Araki, the one man from the village who seemed at all disposed to friendliness with him, regarded him first with disdain, then with amusement, and finally, as the weeks hurried by and Kakichi showed no disposition to be drawn into his plans, with interest.

Araki was a poor soldier; he was complaining and rebellious. He hated the routine and escaped from it whenever he could to the entertainments which his circumstances permitted him to enjoy. There was a house where he might spend pleasant hours with a geisha girl, and where, he told Kakichi, one might relax in a silk kimono and forget the weary round of irksome duties of a soldier's life. Kakichi listened. He had never worn a silk kimono, he laughed. These things would cost him nothing, Araki urged, wanting his companionship. But they were not, Kakichi insisted, things that he wanted, even though they were given him without cost. Araki grew scornful. What would all these books, this Bible, get him? Obedience to discipline could easily be interpreted as a type of subservient meekness, cramping all intelligent initiative. Oh, but he was wrong, Kakichi told him; he who would be a master must first learn well how to serve.

Then there was the incident of the watch. Areki, losing a valuable watch, complained of its loss to the sergeant. Kakichi was questioned. He sent money home every month, and, since the pay was so meager, it was difficult to conceive of where this money could be secured if not by other means. He might have sold the watch. Kakichi listened to the imperious questions of the sergeant with composure. Yes, he admitted, he sent money home; it was needed there. And how, then, did he buy his tobacco and pay for his amusements? He did not buy tobacco, he told them, and his amusements were not of the sort that required money. The sergeant had been quite noisy in his disbelief.

"But this is true!" Kakichi had smiled patiently, suspecting that again the reputation of his family had returned to mock him. "If I were as I was formerly, all might well be as you say. I might very easily then have taken Araki's watch. But I know nothing about it."

And when, in a few days, it was found among Araki's belongings, the attention of the sergeant was centered upon Kakichi quite definitely. There could be no denying the difference of this man from the rest. It might be well to recommend him for promotion. His recommendation was immediately accepted, to Kakichi's surprise and joy.

Araki looked on all this with astonishment, not unmixed with envy. "Is it because of this religious belief of yours that everything is so easy for you?" he wanted to know. "Tell me, Kakichi, is this Bible a difficult book?"

And then it came about that Kakichi, for the first time in his life, was obliged to explain, to one who had more education than he, the principles of his faith. In so doing he found, to his wonderment, that his own comprehension deepened and grew more steady. He became aware of how firmly this faith had become fixed in his life. Hence, out of this incident he was not only strengthened, given a promotion, but he came to secure a friend who was to be invaluable to him in future years.

There were times, however, when his few moments in the day needed to be spent in quiet meditation and prayer. Yoshie had never written very often, but in the spring of the year her letters had unaccountably ceased. His anxiety deepened. In the midst of this new concern, his regiment was dispatched to China, to Tsinan, for the purpose of protecting the lives and possessions of the Japanese living in that district, in the revolution which had begun in 1912 and had continued ever since.

This was the first time he had ever left Japan, and he was filled with deep emotions. When, on the fourth morning, they sighted the spreading, brown China shores, he felt that the world was wide and strange, and all about him were distinct evidences of confusion of tongues, confusion of thought and purpose. Set down in this strange land, in the midst of revolutionary tactics, he noted the writhing, as if in birth, of the new ideas that his superiors hoped to achieve out of all this chaos. They held in view, no doubt, some ordered plan, not so dissimilar in viewpoint from his own plan and that of those who worked with him in his village . . . the peaceful ordering of life that might yield enough food to eat, shelter, and knowledge of a sustaining God. What ordered plan could be brought out of war?

He heard the complaints of the Japanese merchants when the Chinese soldiers looted their shops. He heard the bitter demands of the Chinese that the Japanese evacuate Tsinan. And he heard the cry of the bewildered, poverty-stricken refugees who had neither a place to live nor food to sustain them nor . . . what was worst of all . . . any hope of ever having these things. When he was stationed on guard duty on the docks where they crowded in the bare hope of securing passage out of this country in which there was nothing but continuous warfare and drought, he felt their plight as vitally as his own. Their homes had been destroyed, their crops burned or commandeered for military uses. Japan, with her added development, admittedly superior in modern equipment and advancement, might so easily have come to the help of this, her neighbor, in a cooperation that would be both human and Christian, and whose effect would spread like a radiation of God's kingdom all over a world crying out, not for oppression, but for brotherhood, for love. Everywhere, here, communists and bandits had their way, preying upon the so-called inferiority of the Chinese, inciting them against each other and against Japan, destroying all hope of unity. They were dull, quiescent, these abandoned ones, and some of them lay like bundles of rags for long hours at a time, there in the noise and confusion and filth of the docks, without moving their thin bodies, their eyes closed and their drawn faces covered with the yellow dust of Shantung.

If world history was made up of such events, Kakichi felt that it was little more than a bubble on which all these things—the marches and encounters—were reflected vividly, only to burst into nothingness. War was a result of man's madness, and if this madness was necessary to assure the race a future protection to be brought about through force, then surely there was a great need for the God of love in this world . . . a great need for deep, quiet places in the minds of men, in which strife had no part and the only force was love and human kindliness. Here was a dream all men might unite in dreaming, a prayer all might pray.

These thoughts never left him throughout the summer and autumn months in which he took part in these activities. He knew himself to be fully protected against any possible danger, and the wonder of it grew and grew. But his yearning and anxiety for Yoshie increased. If only he might hear from her! Word came at last, one cold windy day when withdrawal to Tsingtao brought a long-delayed mail. There was no letter from her, but one instead from Mr. Murano. Yoshie had been ill, he wrote, but was improving, although her health still troubled him sorely. The magnificence with which she accomplished things was astonishing . . . was splendid, and no argument could prevail upon her to work less hard. Taiji was so much improved; it was like a miracle. The work on the mountains went on with increasing promise. Even the leper seemed better provided for. And Kokichi had passed away, blessedly, into peace.

Thereafter, as his love and concern for her deepened, Yoshie seemed closer to him in thought than ever before. In his imagination and longing he held her in his arms and comforted her. Her life was his to cherish, and, since he was divided only by the thought of miles, his love and prayers might serve to dissolve these. In the dark, cold nights he yearned to be at home once more, and to see her face.

One night, late in December, he could not sleep. He heard the clock in the guardroom strike one. The reverberation of the whistle of a huge ship coming to dock rattled the windows. The clock struck two. Through the small window beyond his cot he could see the sky, with Orion's brightness lost at moments in thin veils of cloud. Far off in the night a dog barked and a cock anticipated the dawn lustily. There was the sound of footsteps in the hall of the barracks and the chink of an officer's saber as he walked. Kakichi turned restlessly, and then suddenly Yoshie stood beside his cot. He closed his eyes, opening them again to see her even more distinctly. Her slim figure and white face with its soft dark hair outlined clearly against the faint light from the window. He sat up hastily, reaching out his hands to her, his heart beating violently.

"Yoshie!" His lips formed her name and she smiled in answer. All about her was a dim radiance, so that the light from the window was lost in it, and the rest of the long room disappeared in a deep shadow beyond.

"Yoshie! It is you! But how did you get here?"

"Oh, but it is you who have come to me," she answered, and her face was more beautiful than ever he had known it to be, so beautiful that it seemed he could not look upon it without blindness.

"I? I would have wished to come . . . but how could it be so?"

"You could not stay away. In every drop of blood, in every act of life, thinking, breathing, working . . . we are one."

He nodded breathlessly. Tears burned in his eyes. It was like a sacrament of marriage, only far deeper than any sacrament could ever be. There was such a complete oneness as he had never known or dreamed of knowing. He leaned towards her, to stretch out his hands to touch her through the enveloping light. But she was gone. Yet so vivid was the sense of her presence that he lay back, at peace, and fell asleep instantly.

In the morning the sergeant of his platoon handed him a telegram. He stood for a moment staring at it, feeling unaccountably that he knew its message. Slowly his fingers tore open the envelope. It was from Mr. Murano and it read:

"Yoshie entered into eternal rest at three o'clock this morning."

A dreadful sense of loss and desolation oppressed him. He bent over the basin in which he had been washing his face, and, with trembling hands raised the cold water to his eyes. The memory of the past night, and of her words, recurred to him, the sensation of being caught up in the same light that held that precious figure that his hands had not touched. Here was a sacrament not to be dissolved or lost or forgotten. Something of that radiance was upon his face when he raised it once again and went about his duties.

A new urgency now filled his days, an impatience to be at home once again. More than ever now he was convinced that, not through war and revolution, but through the spiritual rebirth of those people at home could the ultimate salvation of his country and of the world be effected. In the hearts of those who would work with love and faith, not for the good of one but for the good of all men, would spring up the streams of living water that would one day overflow the world. His conviction became even more of a certainty with a letter received from Mr. Murano.

"I know," the pastor wrote kindly, "that by this time you have found release from your sorrow in the death of Yoshie. It has been a release that we have all been fortunate in sharing, so that what I have to tell you will seem only a natural result of what, at first, might appear to be meaningless. The work that Yoshie has managed to accomplish, through her sincerity, zeal and self-sacrifice does not now lack for followers and co-operation. Her passing has called the attention of the villagers upon these things, in a manner that her living, so humbly, so unobtrusively, could not do. The fact that she came here unknown and of her own initiative served in the carrying out of our plans and dreams has effected, through her service, a perfectly miraculous response. All things have received an impetus by it. She has aroused not only the love and admiration of these people, but their imagination, so that all we planned now seems in actual process of fulfillment. The results of all this await your return.

"I have been reminded so often in these past days, when her loss seemed so desperately hard to understand, of the words of John: 'Except a grain of wheat fall into the ground and die, it abideth alone, but if it die, it bringeth forth much fruit.'

"Let us then resolve to put forth every effort that this girl's life and service shall not have been in vain, but will bring forth rich fruit in our hearts and in the hearts of all who know her name."

CHAPTER XVII

A GRAIN OF WHEAT

IT WAS A BRIGHT WINTER DAY WHEN KAKICHI AND HIS COM-
rades returned to Tsugu. The village schoolchildren were
all at the boundary line to greet them. The five men who
had all gone into the service at the same time were all
there, but this time Kakichi walked at the head of the
group, since he was the only one who had received a promotion. There were flags and cheers for him in plenty now,
following him all the way to the door of his house, but it
was not these things that warmed his heart so much as the
sight of his mother and brother and sister. Taiji could walk!
And Yuriko had grown so tall and pretty that he scarcely
knew her. His mother's face shone with her love and affec-
tion and pride.

When he entered in at the front door of the shop there
was a new air of order and prosperity, but he went straight
through to the back and out into the clean, swept courtyard. There, in the sun, stood Yoshie's loom, with a piece
of dark blue cloth nearly completed, and the shuttle and
reels just as she had left them. He laid his hand upon it
gently, reminiscently, turning to look into his mother's tear-
filled eyes.

"She spoke your name so often, Kakichi, and said that
she would wait for you on the mountain. She was, indeed,
my daughter, and I loved her dearly and miss her. Yet her
face was so joyous and peaceful at the last that it does not

143

seem fitting to pay reverence to her as one dead. It is as though she has passed into another world and even now remembers us and loves us."

He nodded, rejoicing silently in her belief, for it was one he shared fully. How she, too, had grown!

Mr. Murano came to welcome him that afternoon, and Mata, the latter filled with excited enthusiasm for the co-operatives that were growing steadily into realities. The younger men of the village were more than eager to be put to work on the hills and share in the results. The hermit, too, had returned, delighted to hear of the mountain reforestation, and eager to join in the work.

Mr. Murano suggested that, before Kakichi begin his work in these new tasks awaiting him, the problem of Yoshie's burial should be considered. Her ashes were still on the god-shelf, and it had been Mata's suggestion that they be placed up on the mountain in the midst of the five hundred acres that had been planted since Kakichi's departure. Kakichi looked from one man to the other, deeply moved by their thought. He could have asked for nothing more fitting than this.

"There could be no more perfect memorial for her than the result of her labors," Mr. Murano suggested. "She was an unusual young woman for these days; her life showed the power of a deep faith and an unfailing loyalty. No one could fail to recognize that and be stirred by it."

"And yet she was a person of great simplicity and meekness," Kakichi murmured gently. "She never did these things for reward."

"It is those who accomplish much," Mr. Murano affirmed.

So the next afternoon Kakichi, Mr. Murano, Mata and the hermit, with his dogs, took the winding path up to the hills. Mr. Murano carried the small black urn and Kakichi walked at his side. After the noise and turmoil of the past two years the woods seemed a blessed sanctuary in which his soul might expand, breathe deeply once again and grow. He took deep breaths of the clear air, and as they walked he told them of the observations he had made, and how certain he was that the solution to Japan's problems lay with the people themselves, and that if in each individual consciousness a greater love and greater service could be developed there would be made manifest a resultant power that would effect miracles.

And when, after two hours, they reached that high spot in the hills where now the trees of Yoshie's planting had grown to the height of six feet, they stopped, and in the sunny stillness of the beautiful grove it was this message that Mr. Murano repeated. For others had come to hear. Araki, strangely enough, had followed after them, with a group of people from the village.

A beautiful mountain stream ran through the grove, tumbling over its worn, rocky bed, and beyond its banks upon a higher elevation overlooking the whole broad valley Mata had set up a square shaft with Yoshie's name and age on one side, and on the other the words of John. He repeated them now, and the beauty of the words dropped into each listening heart like a stone into water with ever-widening circles to mark its advent.

" 'Except a grain of wheat fall into the ground and die, it abideth alone, but if it die, it bringeth forth much fruit.' "

While all watched in reverent silence, Mr. Murano performed the simple but beautiful service of placing the ashes in the earth at the foot of the tall shaft. Then, turning to the others, he said: "This hillside, that was bare and waste and rocky, has put forth new life through patient effort. It belongs not to one person alone, but to all who will put forth a similar effort and bring food and life into growth, each man working with his neighbor in unity of faith and purpose. The fruits of our whole life lie within our reach in these hills; the reward of our labors shall be in proportion to that faith. In no other manner can the Kingdom of God come to men in all its abundance."

The hermit raised his head to look down across the rows and rows of chestnut and walnut trees. The dogs lay all about him in the sun.

"I should like to live here," he said. "If I may?"

Mata nodded. "Any man may live here if he wishes and raise those things that will supply food. There are parts of the world, now desert, that were once great forests. If man's intelligence can be brought to bear upon these arid spots, the land will be changed before our eyes, and problems of underproduction and dense city population will be solved. And all these places will be converted from wasteland into beautiful and productive groves such as this, and into fields that will yield their increase."

"All these things can apply likewise to the individual," Kakichi added, and Mr. Murano echoed him. Yes, this was indeed true.

"Here, then, we can let our endeavors, like grains of wheat, grow into fulfillment and replenish the earth and bring contentment to all hearts."

It was late afternoon and the setting sun had turned everything to gold, touching with that same brilliance the faces of this group that knelt in silent prayer on the carpet of fallen leaves. Kakichi again experienced that feeling of ineffable joy and light in the presence of a divine spirit. All seemed to partake of this, and even the chill wind ceased to blow as they remained with bowed heads in the stillness.

Far in the distance could be heard the notes of a temple bell, and far down in the valley the early shadows lay in deep purple pools, shrouded in soft mists. The hills above were blue, then gold, where the light lay upon them. From the forest beyond an owl hooted softly in the early darkness, and swiftly a nightbird cut across the darkening sky. Yet all about them lay a curious brightness that had no part in the setting of the sun.

EPILOGUE

On a summer afternoon, almost three years later, Kakichi stood on the same spot and looked over the hills and
down across the fields to the valley below. It was as though
those early seeds had spread, covering up the bare places
in their path with a new promise, a rich growing. Where
there were open fields he could see men and women working, and hear their voices singing as they worked.

There had been two harvests since he had come back to
take his place as head of the co-operative project on the
mountains. Each industry came under the jurisdiction of a
Co-operative Improvement Association, and each industry
had flourished. They had reaped plentiful rewards from
walnut and chestnut and fig trees. They had harvested not
rice alone, but millet and buckwheat, corn and potatoes.
Mata's old mill and another new one ground wheat into
flour. There was bread now to be bought and sold. The
co-operatives had supplied each one of their members with
five head of sheep and some chickens, giving each man no
more than he could reasonably care for. There were eggs to
be used and sold; there was wool for clothing. There was
new food to be eaten, food on which they thrived. Kakube-e had undertaken the raising of pigs and the curing
of hams and bacon and had been most successful. There
were fish hatcheries in the shallow streams, and hives of bees
to be cared for by those who were crippled. Taiji had become experienced at this occupation and was happily sharing his experience with others. Chief among these were

the two sons of the leper, who had died. Dr. Kurino had found good homes for the children.

Kakichi's heart was exultant as he rehearsed in his mind the tremendous progress that had evolved out of these years. There was food, and enough, now; there was contentment too. Men thought of peace, not of war; they shared and exchanged with their neighbors . . . they grew, because all about them was the constant stimulation of growth. No one was utterly dependent upon rice or the doubtful sale of silkworms. Each season supplied its reward, as each prayer its fulfillment.

In the village there were cooking schools and classes in diversified farming. The Temperance Society was an established thing and Araki was now its enthusiastic leader. Although no one had been asked to attend Mr. Murano's meetings and classes, they had grown and were ever growing, so that the small room had long since been abandoned for a larger place in which to worship. There was an efficient Credit Association and the Land Improvement Cooperative took care of all experimental work on the farms.

Kakichi drew a deep breath. He would never cease, as he breathed, to give thanks. His gratitude rose like incense night and day, as the smoke rose from the chimneys of his own house and scores of other houses, where there was neither starvation nor retrogression. There were more eyes turned to the hills from which had come their help. Those early prayers of a few had deepened from a tiny stream to a great river spreading in beauty to a vast sea in which one was not lost, but taken into oneness of thought and purpose and lifted up once again to drop as inspired thought into the hearts of those who came to look and remained to live and to work. In other communities similar projects were commencing to grow and to flourish.

All things had become new! The thought lifted his heart like a song. There was newness of life for him, too. Young people came sometimes to be married here on this hillside, before the memorial to Yoshie, feeling, no doubt, the added consecration of that one whose unselfish spirit had been the seed from which all this abundance had come. Some day soon, Kakichi thought wistfully, he, too, might be wed here in this blessed spot. That, he knew, would be Yoshie's wish for him, and he knew he must obey that wish. He thought of Hana, whom he had met on that evening so long ago when he had first attended Mr. Murano's meeting. She had worked in the Post Office then, but she worked now with Yuki and Yuriko in the cooking school classes that had been formed with such success in the village. She, too, had loved Yoshie, and this had drawn her and Kakichi closer together. She was good and beautiful; his thoughts reached out to her in longing and he was joyous in the knowledge of her love.

All about him the sun lay with a golden light upon wide fields and great acres of trees, upon those same trees which Yoshie had planted. Kakichi looked upon them, knowing them to be not unlike his own life, his own work, and the lives and labors of all who gave these things into eternal hands for growth and guidance. Their branches bent now, in the sunny stillness, with the weight of their richly abundant fruit.